Dear Reader,

I love cowboys. In Tucker Lambert, you'll find the quintessential American cowboy. He's a drifter-turned-rancher with a history of being down on his luck and a habit of breaking hearts. It takes a lot of man to rise above that track record then recognize and help heal a heart that's even more bruised and battered than his own. And it takes a lot of woman (as Sara Stewart is) to risk getting involved with a man like Tucker.

I love these characters for both their strength and their weaknesses and for their ability to balance passion and compassion and find their way to each other. With Texas, a land as wild and reckless as their love story, for a backdrop, I hope you'll find their story as compelling to read as it was for me to write!

My very best to you,

Cindy Gerard

GREATEST TEXAS LOVE STORIES OF ALL TIME

★
GREATEST
TEXAS LOVE STORIES
OF ALL TIME

THE COWBOY TAKES A LADY
Cindy Gerard

He's a Cowboy!

Silhouette Books

Published by Silhouette Books
America's Publisher of Contemporary Romance

SILHOUETTE BOOKS

ISBN 0-373-65225-9

THE COWBOY TAKES A LADY

This edition published by arrangement with Harlequin Books S.A.

® and TM are trademarks of Harlequin Books S.A., used under license.
Trademarks indicated with ® are registered in the United States Patent
and Trademark Office, the Canadian Trade Marks Office and in other
countries.

Visit Silhouette at www.eHarlequin.com

Printed in U.S.A.

CINDY GERARD

If asked "What's your idea of heaven?" Cindy Gerard would say a warm sun, a cool breeze, pan pizza and a good book. If she had to settle for one of the four, she'd opt for the book, with the pizza running a close second. Inspired by the pleasure she's received from the books she's read and her longtime love affair with her husband, Tom, Cindy now creates her own evocative and sensual love stories about compelling characters and complex relationships.

This bestselling author of close to twenty books has received numerous industry awards, among them the National Readers' Choice Award, multiple *Romantic Times* nominations and two RITA® Award nominations from the Romance Writers of America. Cindy loves to hear from her readers and invites them to visit her Web page at www.tlt.com/authors/cgerard.htm.

This book is dedicated to bad seeds everywhere
and to the women who find the good in them.

One

She'd been warned about men like him. She'd been warned about this man specifically. Keep your distance, Karla had told her. Tucker Lambert was bad.

But, oh, Sara thought, watching him through twenty yards of moonlight and the heat of the sultry Texas night, *was he pretty...*

He hadn't heard her slip outside. Standing with his back to her, he didn't know she was studying him as he folded his arms across the top board of the paddock fence. And while his loose-hipped cowboy stance appeared posed, he couldn't possibly be aware of the picture he made.

A full, rising moon cast his body in dramatic relief against a sweeping vista dotted with the dark silhouettes of a dozen placidly grazing horses. Thinking himself alone, he contemplated the night in silence.

The silence, she decided, watching him from the shadows of the covered courtyard entry of the little guest casa, wasn't the only thing they would share before the night was over.

Tucker Lambert. The quintessential American cowboy. He was a drifter turned rancher with a history of being down on his luck and a habit of breaking hearts. A real Walkaway Joe...exactly the kind of man Sara Stewart needed tonight.

He'd tossed his sweat-stained chambray shirt carelessly over the white rail fence beside him. His workingman's jeans, covered with dust and frayed at one knee, rode low and loose on his lean hips. A battered gray Resistol sat far back on his head. Beneath it, his thick chamois-colored hair was matted with sweat, spiked in soft, damp curls at the nape of his neck.

Pretty, she thought again, appreciating the deep tan of his bare back, painted even darker by the moonglow, the toned muscle tapering to a narrow waist, defined by shadows and substance. Like a statue cast in bronze, he was lovingly molded, artfully crafted. Perfection. Temptation. As faultless in design as he was flawed in character.

Karla had called him a womanizer, yet smiled fondly when she said it. He was a man who played at love and loved to play, she'd said. A man who had broken more hearts in his thirty-plus years than he had broncs. A man you could count on for only one thing—to leave you as he'd found you. Alone.

Slipping open another button on her scoop-necked gauze blouse, Sara pressed the cool, sweating long-neck against her heated skin before tipping the bottle to her mouth and taking another deep swallow.

If Karla was here, she'd tell her gently that she'd had too much to drink. Pragmatist that she was, Sara would concur. She'd even agree that sometimes these days she drank a little too much, a little too often. After all, that was the reason Karla and Lance had shanghaied her seven long days ago and dumped her in this godforsaken sweat hole Lambert called a ranch in the first place.

What they didn't understand was that when she drank, she did it for a reason. It helped her forget. At least it helped her forget some things. Oddly enough, it helped her remember others. It helped her remember what was real and at the same time let her forget she didn't deserve any better than what she was getting. And tonight, it had played a major part in convincing her that Tucker Lambert, her reluctant nurse-maid and a man who until a week ago had been a stranger, was as good a distraction as any to buffer another kind of pain.

She slumped back against the stone-and-adobe archway as a picture flashed through her mind with the force of an ax blow. The face of a child, nameless, bloodless, except for the deep crimson stain spread across his chest. Another life she couldn't save.

Forcing the gruesome picture from her mind, she battled back the ache of failure and the hollow hope-lessness that came with it. She didn't need a doctor to diagnose her problem. Battle fatigue. Too many years working as head nurse in ER. Too much blood. Too much violence. Too much death. Too much hope lost for this healer who couldn't always heal.

She refused to think about any of that now. After all, Karla and Lance had brought her here so that she could get away from the front line. And, she reminded herself staunchly as she focused on Lambert again, tonight's plan was to concentrate on him. She was determined to do just that. He was going to be her fix. At least for tonight. He was a temporary man. She needed a temporary relief. It was a winning combination if she'd ever seen one.

Shoving away from the archway, she dragged a hand through the tousled brown hair that barely skimmed her shoulders and walked with slow determination toward him. The soft folds of her long print skirt brushed sensually against her bare legs with each step. The dry Texas dust, still warm from the blistering summer sun, sifted like fine powder between her bare toes.

Lambert angled his head around when he heard her approach. With a sleepy blink of his blue eyes, he looked her up and down as she pressed her shoulder blades against the wooden fence rail beside him.

She let him look. Showing him her profile, she stared first at the little guest casa she'd been forced to temporarily call home, then at the matching dwelling Lambert's brother shared with his wife and child and finally at the dim lights of the sprawling Spanish ranch house nestled between them.

Aware that he was still watching her, she drew the bottle across her throat, then downward in a slow cooling glide. Holding it lingeringly between her breasts, she invited his gaze to follow.

"Hot," she said, hearing a huskiness in her voice that his bold assessment created.

"Texas," he said, after a long, slow eyeful. "July," he added, turning back to his study of the night and hiking a boot heel on the bottom fence rung. "Kind of tells the tale, don't it?"

She forced a laugh. "You like to play the good ol' boy, don't you?" Tipping her head back, she gazed up at the dazzling stars. They lit up the night on the plains as they never could in the smog-drenched Dallas skies she was used to. "You like to come across as the uneducated cowpoke who's never read anything but a cutting-horse journal or the label on a longneck."

He sliced her a lazy, sideways glance. "And what do *you* like to play, Miz Stewart? Other than the wounded bird, that is."

Coated in his soft Texas drawl, his barb lost enough of its sting that she smiled again. So, the cowboy had an opinion. So what? She told herself she didn't care what he thought of her. She didn't want to get to know him well enough to have it matter. Her tone said as much. "Is that how you see me?"

He turned to fully face her then. Thumbing back his hat, he leaned an elbow on the fence railing. "I see you as a woman with a problem." He glanced pointedly at the bottle in her hand before he met her eyes again. "And it seems to me that you're lookin' in the wrong place for the answer."

She drew a deep breath, determined not to let his words get to her. "Well, now, that's where your Will Rogers philosophy has let you down, cowboy." Defiant, she took a long, deep swallow. Amber courage. Liquid oblivion. "Because, you see, Mr. Lambert, I'm not looking for any answers."

His response was swift and painfully on target. "Hidin' away from 'em, then."

She closed her eyes, wanting to hate him for being right, hate herself for what she was doing. But as it had so often lately, the bottle had become her security. She laid it again to the side of her face, catching the last beads of cooling sweat against her cheek as a teardrop of perspiration trickled between her breasts.

She breathed deep of a night that was scented with dry sage and Texas heat. "I didn't come out here to be analyzed."

"Is that a fact?" His lazy question was soft and slow and judgmental. "Then why exactly *did* you come out here, Miz Stewart...ma'am?" he added with deliberate provocation.

She turned toward him. His eyes were narrowed and searching. Even in the moonlight, they were a stunning, sultry blue. Even beneath the shadowed brim of his hat, she could see the dare—sexual, mocking, dangerous.

Karla was right. He was bad. She wanted him tonight in spite of it. She *needed* him tonight because of it.

Boldly holding his gaze, she moved toward him, then against him. Lifting her hand to his face, she caressed his jaw with the cool side of the bottle in a slow, intimate enticement.

He didn't move. Not away from her. Not into her. He just stood there, waiting in a silence that could have been either anticipation or indifference.

"Why did I come out here?" she murmured, hooking her wrist behind his neck and pulling herself flush against him. "If you can't figure it out…then you're not the man I thought you were."

He was hot. The burn of his bare chest seared through the thin cotton of her blouse where her breasts pressed and pulsed against him. Beneath her hand, she felt a sheen of sweat coating his back. It made her wonder at the taste of him. And at the extent of his hunger.

She lowered her mouth to touch and tease her lips across the pulsebeat at his throat—and tasted salt, and musk, and male.

He sucked in his breath. The sinewy cords of his neck grew taut and ridged before he raised his hands to grip her wrists. Strong hands. Workingman's hands. Yet remarkably gentle as he tugged them slowly from around his neck and held them steady between their bodies.

"Why, Miz Stewart…" His voice, southern-soft and midnight-mellow, had a distinctly rusty edge. "I do believe you plan to have your way with me."

He was six-two to her five-three. He outweighed her by a good seventy pounds. In a test of strength, she'd lose, hands down. But this wasn't about strength. It was about sex and salvation and a few stunning hours of oblivion.

She looked directly into his eyes. The shadow of his Resistol hardened the dark expression on his face as she pulled her wrists free of his grip and moved into him again.

"My way… Your way…" The bottle slid through her fingers and dropped with a muffled thump to the ground. "Any way you want, cowboy," she whispered against his throat as her hands glided along the damp satin of his back, then slipped to his lean hips. With a boldness born of determination, she cupped the tight, taut muscle of his buttocks in her palms.

She felt him shudder when she pulled him flush against her hips. Felt the deep rise and fall of his chest, the thick heavy thuds of his heartbeat against her breasts.

"You like that." Her smile pressed to his bare chest as the swift and hard length of his arousal nestled in the softness of her belly. "For a minute there, I thought you were going to disappoint me."

A low, deep chuckle rumbled against her cheek. "Oh, sweetheart, I'm going to disappoint you, all right." His warm breath fanned the top of her head. "Bank on it."

"Now, that's where you're wrong again." She arched her neck to look up at him. "Nothing you could do could disappoint me. Unless you told me you didn't want to take me to bed.''

He drew a deep, ragged breath. Then he gripped her hard by her shoulders and set her away. ''And that's all you want from me?''

The barely controlled anger in his voice surprised her. So did the roughness of his hold. His fingers bit into her shoulders. When she flinched, grimacing at the unexpected pain, he let her go.

''That's all I want,'' she assured him, unsettled by the turmoil in his eyes, but determined to go through with this. ''No commitments. No expectations. Just a good time. You can live with that, can't you?''

His eyes turned dark and brooding. ''I can live with it,'' he said with grim intensity. ''The question is, can you?''

This was something she hadn't expected from him. Hesitation. Anger. Maybe even a conscience. She didn't want any part of any of it. And she didn't want to think about the fact that he might be right. That she might not be able to live with herself if she saw this through. She didn't want to think at all. After months of existing in an enforced, protective numbness, she wanted to feel.

''For a man who's noted for action,'' she murmured, hating the telling tremor in her voice, ''you ask an awful lot of questions.''

''And for a woman who's already got one problem, you're taking a foolish risk, asking for another.''

She resented the hell out of the pity she read in his

eyes. Resented it and refused to let it affect her. Her problems were hers, no one else's. Especially not his.

She didn't understand his reaction. The general consensus was that Lambert was a bad seed with the morals of an alley cat and the scruples of a grifter.

"No problem, Tucker," she said, banking on his reputation as truth. "And no complications. I promise. Just tonight. I'm only asking for tonight." She swallowed hard, hating herself for letting the pleading note creep into her voice, hoping he didn't recognize it for what it was.

But he recognized her desperation. And in the moment before he surrendered to it, she sensed that at some time in his life he had felt it, too, and had suffered its debilitating power.

Moonlight gilded the hard planes of his face as he caught her shoulders in his hands and drew her toward him. Starlight reflected in the blue eyes that searched hers with a painfully searing intensity. And the night sounds, as soulful and lonely as the look on his face, blended with his tortured groan as he brought his mouth to hers.

The hesitation ended then. He took her mouth with the fierceness of a warrior, with the sureness of a conqueror. No slow introduction. No sweet seduction. Openmouthed, hot and demanding, he slanted his mouth across hers, offering no options, making no allowances.

Punishing and rough, erotic and exciting, his kiss was the beginning of the escape she needed. And she told herself this was what she wanted. All the power, all the fury, all the promise of losing herself in his fire.

She wrapped her arms around his neck, clinging to him, her open mouth accommodating his demands, desperate for his tongue and his taste and the savage sexual healing his explosive passion promised.

"Where?" she whispered, breathless and yearning when he came up for air.

He didn't answer. Just clenched his jaw, lifted her against him and started walking. She buried her face against his shoulder, wrapped her legs around his waist and hung on for the ride.

This was what she wanted, she assured herself, as excitement blended with fear, then blurred unexpectedly into shame. This was what she needed. To be lost in something more powerful than pain. To enjoy, if only for the moment, the honesty of lust, the false intimacy of physical love that would end long before sunrise.

His booted footsteps echoed against the floor of the brick-and-tile courtyard as he carried her under the archway. The screen door creaked, then slammed shut behind them as he shouldered his way inside the small casa that had been both her home and her prison for the past week.

Draped in darkness, wrapped in his heat and the scent of aggressive, aroused male, it took a moment for her to realize he was urging her to let go. Another moment before she became aware that they were in her bedroom, standing beside her bed.

Slowly, she unwrapped her legs from around him.

Slower still, she unwound her arms from around his neck.

A sharp, stark stab of panic swamped her again. What was she doing? What had she come to? This wasn't her. This wasn't right.

But this was real, she reminded herself, battling the feeling back. And it was vital. The physical rush she felt in Lambert's arms reminded her that she was a living, breathing woman who had functioned too long in the drugging fog of nothingness.

With a shaking hand, she reached up and tugged the hat from his head. With a tremulous breath, she tossed it to the floor.

As still as the silence, he watched her. As illicit as the original sin, he tempted her. His only reaction was the tight clenching of his jaw, the accelerated pulse-beat that raced with anticipation at his throat.

Her hand was way past trembling when she reached for him. She touched her fingers to his jaw, then ran them through the lush, damp gold of his hair. Closing her eyes, she trailed spread palms down the light dusting of curls covering his chest, then lower.

The fine curling hair on his belly tickled the back of her hands when she reached for his silver belt buckle. The flat muscles of his abdomen tightened with his indrawn breath, just as her chest tightened with anticipation and need. And as she closed her fingers over the buckle and tugged it free, she felt his heartbeat quicken with hers.

In a lightning move, his hands covered hers, stilling them.

Her head snapped back. For a moment, in the shadowed darkness, she could have sworn she saw denial in his eyes. The shock was quick, the disappointment cutting. Then she reminded herself who she was with and smiled at her own naiveté. This was Tucker Lambert. This was the love-'em-and-leave-'em legend of the Texas sage. How had Karla summed him up? *Quick with a grin, time to kill, women to win.*

"What's the matter, Lambert?" she said huskily, baiting him. "Am I going too fast for you?"

He slowly shook his head as a smile that held less humor than it did grim restraint lifted one corner of his mouth. "Oh, sweetheart, if you only knew...."

Before she lost her nerve, her hands moved again to his buckle. "I want to know, Tucker. Word has it you're just the man to fill me in."

Again his strong hands stopped her.

"Ladies first," he insisted when she raised her gaze to his questioningly.

Bold in the darkness, foolishly discounting the thought that she was about to make love to a man she barely knew, she met his challenge. "Then by all means..." She reached behind her, gripped the corner post of the four-poster bed at her back with trembling hands and leaned against it. "You do the honors." Her throat was so tight it came out as a raspy whisper.

Without a word, he leaned over to turn on a bedside lamp. Pale lampglow cast soft shadows over the room—and too much light on the reality of what was about to happen.

His sleepy gaze dropped to her breasts, where her

blouse stretched tight across them. She felt her nipples harden under his bold stare, and knew by his deep, shimmering breath that the soft cotton gave away her body's response.

"This particular stage of the game," he said, watching her face as he cocked one knee and hooked his thumbs in his belt loops, "I prefer to enjoy as a spectator."

His intent couldn't have been clearer. He wanted her to strip for him. Shame almost got the best of her then. Shame and indecision. She hadn't planned on this. She hadn't planned on having to think about what she was doing, or that she'd have the presence of mind to try to talk herself out of it.

What she'd planned on was a few hours of dark, mindless sex. No promises. No regrets. The price of a condom seemed a fair exchange for her pride.

But suddenly her pride and her brazen disregard for the values she'd lived by all her life seemed a high price after all. He must have read the indecision on her face in that moment before she remembered that she had little pride left to hold on to…and that her values had already been discounted by events over which she had no control.

One corner of that teasing, tempting mouth tipped up in a mocking grin. "Well, now… What's this? A change of heart?"

He was laughing at her. And why not? She was a joke.

"Change of heart?" she echoed, with a lift of her chin and a renewed resolve to see this through. This might be a real low point in her life, but she'd be damned if she'd come this far and miss out on the punch line.

Clawing her way out of the depression that haunted her, she met his taunting gaze with defiance. ''My heart has nothing to do with what I want from you. And I'm told that what I want—'' she paused, wet her lips and flicked open another button on her blouse ''—is something you've had lots of practice giving.''

He stood motionless as she undid the last button. Didn't so much as blink as she shrugged the gauzy cotton from her shoulders. Her heart stalled, then battered her breast, as she bared herself to the lamplight and the last of her pride to his burning gaze.

Before she lost her nerve, she unbuttoned her skirt and stepped out of it. Her chest hurt, her throat felt as raw as her nerves as she stood before him, naked except for her panties and the light dusting of Texas sand on her bare feet.

And still he stood there.

''Don't tell me you're not up to it.'' She was taunting him, wishing she had something stronger than her courage to help her see this through.

He took a slow, stalking step toward her. Stopping mere inches away, he searched her face, then raised his hand and brushed his knuckles in a soft, sensual caress across her jaw.

She trembled and, with a boldness that sent her heart racing, cupped his hand in hers and guided it slowly to her breast.

Her breath stalled, thick and aching, as his big

hand, hot and callused and blatantly possessive, closed around her. She swayed against the heat of his touch, her eyes drifting shut as he kneaded her softly, and then, with a groan that could have been desperation or desire, dragged her roughly against him.

His open belt buckle bit into the sensitive skin of her hip as he lifted her off her feet. The corded muscle of his arms held her steady and strong as he carried her out of the room.

An unsolicited surge of panic swamped her as she looked over his shoulder. "I don't know what you've got in mind...but the bed's back there."

"And the shower's in here," he said. Letting her body slide in a slow, sensuous glide against him, he lowered her to her feet in the middle of the tub.

With a smile as tempting as it was wicked, he reached for the faucet—and turned on the cold water full blast.

Liquid ice hit her full in the face. She sucked in a sharp breath, then shrieked at him, jolted out of shock mode and into rage. "What—what·the hell are you doing!"

"Just giving you a chance to cool off, Miz Stewart," he said in a maddeningly placating tone as she scrambled to get away. "A chance to cool off and sober up," he added, his voice growing strained as she fought him.

"You b-b-bastard!"

"So some say."

She screamed then. And swung. And kicked with everything that was in her. Dodging her clubbing fists and ignoring her bloodcurdling oaths, he held her where she stood with an ease that sent her into an even wilder rage.

She had the supreme satisfaction of hearing his grunt of pain when one of her fists connected with his jaw.

"Just hold still now, and get it over with. Believe me, you'll thank me for this in the morning."

She glared at him through a thick curtain of water-soaked hair. "I'll thank you to get the hell out of here!"

When he didn't budge, she called him every ugly name she could summon up from her vocabulary. When he covered her mouth with his broad palm, she bit him.

He yelped and jerked his hand away. Ducking another uppercut, he moved in on her, pinioning her arms behind her back. "If you'd stay the hell put, I'd let you go," he growled, forcing her under the spray again. "Just settle down. If you promise to be good…"

"I'll promise you n-nothing," she gasped, spitting water and shaking with fury. "Let…me…go, you… you sorry s-son of a bitch!"

"Careful, careful… All this sweet talk'll turn my head."

His chuckle infuriated her beyond the point of control. She bucked and twisted and reared back until they were both in danger of falling. Finally giving up, he released her and backed a healthy step toward the door.

She hurled a bar of soap at him. Then a bottle of shampoo. He ducked, but not in time. The plastic bottle grazed his shoulder, then bounced off the wall to land on the floor. He stopped abruptly, his face darkening with a swift loss of patience. In two long strides, he stalked back to the shower.

He caught her swinging fists in midair, banded both wrists behind her back and dragged her roughly against him. "When you decide you want to talk about what's eating you up from inside," he demanded, his mouth an inch away from hers, "let me know. And when you make that decision, you make damn sure you come to me sober."

Ignoring the shower spray, her wet, shivering body and her vivid curses, he pinned her with his gaze. "And one more thing…if you come to me again looking for what you were looking for tonight, don't count on a replay of this little shower scene. Next time, you're going to get exactly what you asked for."

Nose to nose with him, she stared him down, determined that he'd see none of her humiliation and all of her anger.

"I wouldn't come to you for—"

He cut her words off with his mouth, and with a kiss that was as disabling as his arms were strong around her.

It started out with one intent. To overpower. To dominate. To make a liar out of her anger. Bruising and rough, punishing and possessing, he kissed her the way he had outside in the moonlight. Yet when she murmured in surrender and sagged against him in defeat, instead of taking advantage, he eased his hold.

The kiss was transformed, in a subtle, sensual heartbeat, to something generous and giving, soft and healing. As gentle as the hand that brushed the wet hair away from her eyes. As tender as the callused thumb that stroked her jaw. So gentle, it made her weak. So tender, it made her want to cry.

Slowly, slowly, he pulled away, watching her face all the while. Defenseless against the compassion in his eyes and a damnable rush of tears she refused to shed, she lowered her head.

"I hate you." It came out as a raw, reedy whisper as she fought a bewildering tangle of anger and need.

He let go of a deep, labored breath. "Yeah, well, that was the idea."

The gentleness in his tone brought her head up.

"Seemed to me you needed someone to hate a little more than you hate yourself at the moment," he said, answering her unasked question. "But I figure you'll get over it. And I figure I'll survive if you don't."

She didn't cover herself when he just stood there. Didn't fight him when he cupped his palm around the nape of her neck. Didn't resist when he drew her toward him again.

And she told herself she didn't let her tears fall when he touched her mouth with a soft, almost apologetic kiss before he left her...shivering, shamed and alone.

Two

Sucking in a deep draft of air, Tucker let the door shut softly behind him. Hands on his hips, head lowered, he stood in the archway, waiting for the fist that had clenched in his gut to let go.

Hell. He didn't need this. He didn't like it. And he sure as the devil didn't understand it. He'd left women crying before. And, yeah, it had bothered him. But not like this. Never like this.

He didn't even know the woman. He told himself he didn't want to know her. He was just putting up with her as a favor to Karla and Lance.

"Some favor," he grumbled darkly, knowing he'd go to the limit not to compromise one of the few friendships he valued. Walking away from Sara Stewart was a case in point. She and her pleading brown eyes had stretched the hell out of that limit tonight.

If it wasn't for Karla and Lance, he'd turn on his heel, stalk back in there and give the lady what she wanted. Hadn't *she* come looking for *him?* Hadn't *she* been the one doing the seducing?

He jammed his hat tighter on his head and swore. She was an adult. She was willing. And, sweet Lord, he wanted her. Even though he'd had little or no contact with her during the seven days and nights since she'd come to Blue Sky, it had been damn hard not to want her. He had eyes. Even from a distance he could see that she was all soft feminine heat and sweet sexy curves. But Karla had warned him to leave her alone, so he had. Until tonight, she'd made it easy. Until tonight, she'd kept to herself.

Until tonight.

He swore again and scowled at the night sky. Tonight never would have happened if it hadn't been for his kid brother. He sucked in another deep breath as he thought of Tag and his wife, Lana, and the sexual byplay that had shimmered on the air between them at supper. Damn kids. They were barely twenty. Baby Cody was a little over two years old, Lana was pregnant again, and they still didn't have the sense to keep their hands off each other.

All those hot looks and soft touches passing between them at the supper table tonight had gotten to him. Knowing that the minute Cody was down for the night, they'd headed for their own bed, for anything but sleep, had had Tucker restless and edgy.

And wanting. And stalking outside into the moonlight.

All he'd wanted was some fresh air and some distance from Tag and Lana's casa, where his brother was getting some of what Sara Stewart had just offered him.

A shaft of desire shot straight and sharp to his groin as he remembered how she'd looked when she came to him. She'd been a poor boy's fantasy, propositioning him by moonglow. A weak man's downfall, pleading with him by lamplight. Lamplight that had spilled and caressed and shadowed her small, lush curves and pale, flawless skin.

Her thick chestnut hair had tumbled wantonly over soulful brown eyes that were both prideful and needy. Her breasts were small and high, tipped with the prettiest, poutiest nipples. Pressed against his palm, she'd been a quivering, velvet handful. Taken inside his mouth, she'd have been a sweet, delicate mouthful. And he had no doubt that if he'd sank inside her sleek, tight heat, she would have sheathed and clenched and milked his burning flesh until he was drained of everything but ragged breaths and thundering heartbeats.

He scuffed a boot heel against the worn tile floor of the patio and worked his jaw. He still couldn't believe he'd said no. Still couldn't believe that the pain she'd been too proud to admit to had touched him. In the dark, in her arms, he'd hurt for her. In the heat, in the moment, he'd cared about her. But the worst part was that as he stood there, watching her strip away her pride along with her clothes, he'd been the one who felt exposed.

In a sharp and unforgiving moment of insight, he'd seen a glimpse of himself in her desperation. He'd seen himself as a man who'd always wanted more and settled for less. He'd seen a man hoping that sex would hide, if not heal, his own hurt.

The self-discovery had hit him like a kick from a rank mount. He was still reeling from the impact. It had scared the hell out of him to see both himself and her motives so clearly. In the moment when she stood before him, naked and needy, pleading and exposed, he'd come close to hating her. Not for what she was doing to herself, but for making him see how shallow his own life had become.

He was thirty-two years old, a busted-up cowboy, with Tag, Lana and little Cody the family he claimed, and a bastard of an old man drifting around Texas that he didn't. He had a gross of partying buddies and too few good friends. There weren't enough hours in each day to get his work done or to make up for all the years he'd wasted. If that wasn't enough to keep him awake at night, he had a mortgage the size of the moon, and the knowledge that his kid brother was counting on him to keep roofs over all their heads.

He didn't need Sara Stewart to add to an already full plate. He sure as hell didn't need her messing with his head. If he had taken her tonight, he'd have had nothing to feel guilty about. Women had used him as often as he'd used them. The fact that they could have used each other mutually should have been reason enough to sanction one more go-round.

And yet he'd walked away.

He cursed again under his breath and stalked through the dust to the ranch house. He'd picked a hell of a fine time to recognize that sex was not what either of them really needed.

"It's not gonna work," Tucker stated flatly and firmly into the phone three hours later.

"What— Who is this?"

Tucker envisioned Karla Griffin all snug and comfy in her bed. Her dark Spanish eyes would be heavy with sleep, her tumble of long black hair tangled and falling over her face. Beside her, Lance would be slowly rousing and wondering what low-life slug was bothering his wife at 3:00 a.m.

"Wake up, Karla," Tucker ordered without sympathy, taking perverse satisfaction in knowing he wasn't the only one losing sleep over Sara Stewart. "This is the nursemaid, darlin', and I'm calling to turn in my shingle."

"Tucker?"

"Yeah, it's Tucker, and you need to listen to me. You've got to come and get her."

"What's wrong?" Karla was awake now. He could hear the worry that had edged into her soft voice. Good. She ought to be worried. "Tucker...what have you done?"

He muttered an oath. What had he done? One of the few noble acts he'd ever committed in his sad, sorry life, that was what he'd done. He'd walked away from a willing woman. Willing, wanton, and as needy for a tumble as any woman he'd ever seen.

He pinched the bridge of his nose between finger and thumb to stall the throbbing that had taken up residence there. Shaking off another tug of empathy for the spitfire who'd called him everything but dirt, he focused in on his mission again.

"I haven't done anything. Yet," he added in warning. "But she's going to get exactly what she's asking for if you don't get her out of my hair."

"Problem, Tucker?" This from Lance, who had picked up on the other extension.

Cutting to the meat of the matter was both Lance's style and his strength. He was the CEO of one of the biggest corporations in Texas, a sucker for his wife, and, due to an ironic twist of fate, Tucker's friend and business partner in his cutting-horse operation.

"Yeah, I've got a problem. One that's about five foot three inches tall and, judging from an earlier encounter, I'd say about one-ten soaking wet." He worked to keep a repeat of a vivid, erotic picture of that soaking-wet, naked woman from drifting through his mind again. "And she comes equipped with a bulldogger's mouth, and all the charm of a cactus."

"So what I'm hearing," Lance said, measuring his words, "is that you've finally met a woman you can't handle." It wasn't a question. It was an amused and curious commentary.

Tucker rubbed his jaw where her small fist had connected, then gauged the depth of the teeth marks in the fleshy part of his palm. "You think this is funny. Fine. Think what you want. But I don't deserve this, buddy."

"Maybe not, but she deserves a chance to get herself back together."

Tucker slumped back in the chair, rubbing the flat of his hand across his bare belly. He stared wearily at the clock on the wall and let out a tired sigh. He had to be in the saddle in three hours.

"Look. I'm sorry for what she's been through. I'm sorry she's in bad shape. But she's not my problem, dammit. I've got a ranch to run. I've got a dozen competitions to get ready for, that blockhead two-year-old of yours to break, and Jas Carsten's mare to polish. I can't do any of it if I've got to play watchdog to a problem drinker."

"She's not a problem drinker, Tucker," Karla interjected in a bid for understanding. "She just needs rest. She'll be fine as soon as she starts thinking straight again."

Tucker knew Sara Stewart's story. Better than he wanted to, which probably accounted for his actions tonight. She was an uptown girl, born and bred to privilege, like Lance. But she'd wanted to make a difference, so she'd bucked her daddy's wishes that she marry well to become a nurse instead—which, as far as Tucker was concerned, proved she was not only mule-headed, but stupid.

According to Karla, the years of working ER in a Dallas trauma center had taken their toll. Rather than admit the stress was getting to her and request lighter duty, Sara had thrown herself deeper into the action. It had finally caught up to her. Unable to combat the emotional turmoil building inside her, she'd burned out. She'd turned to booze to help her cope a little too often. This enforced exile to Blue Sky, Tucker's ranch, was supposed to provide Sara with a time-out, away from the city and the ER.

Well, one thing was for sure, Tucker thought as he looked out the window into the vast and empty night. Blue Sky was away from the city. The cutting-horse ranch was situated on the edge of Nowhere, Texas, close enough to San Antonio to make it possible to stock supplies and far enough to guarantee privacy. Its location gave a man plenty of time to work without distraction. But it gave a woman with a problem too much time to get herself into a whole heap more trouble.

Her little performance tonight was a case in point. With a clear head, that little city girl would never have looked twice at a rounder like him, let alone beg him to take her to bed.

"Look," he began, feeling his body stir at the memory and needing to squelch it, "I know I owe you—"

"Whoa. You owe me nothing," Lance stated firmly, cutting him off.

Tucker knew different. He owed Lance big-time. If not for Lance and his financial backing, Blue Sky would still be a distant, impossible dream and Tucker would still be drifting from one dead-end job to another. Plus, his brother would still be working road construction while his wife and baby struggled along without him, waiting to see him on infrequent weekends home.

"You're working like a dog down there," Lance continued when Tucker remained silent. "And you're making my investment pay. This has nothing to do with debt. It has to do with friendship. Sara needs help."

"Then send her to one of those fancy clinics where she can be pampered and placated and pumped full of TLC," he grumbled, fighting a persistent empathy for a woman he didn't even want to like. "She can afford it. Even if she couldn't, you can. If she's your friend, you ought to do that for her."

"It's because we are her friends that we brought her to Blue Sky, Tuck." Karla's plea dug even deeper than it had when she asked for his help to begin with. He'd always been an easy target for Karla. She knew just how to hit his bull's-eye. She also knew he was no good, and loved him like a brother in spite of it.

"She just needs some space," she went on. "A place to sort this out. In her own time. In her own way."

Tucker clenched his jaw and saw Sara, by moonlight. *Her own way* was going to kill him—or geld him, he thought grimly as her dark eyes and slight, sexy little body again came vividly to mind. A few more encounters like tonight's and he'd meet with a slow and painful end.

"Yeah, well, don't hold me responsible if she decides to cut and run," he grumbled, pinning a barrelful of hope on her hightailing it away from Blue Sky because of that little scene they hadn't quite played out.

"She won't." Karla's voice was soft but full of conviction, gunning down Tucker's hope like a sharp-shooter picking off beer bottles. "She promised me she'd stay put and work on this. She won't break that promise.

"Tucker," she added after a long pause. "Please. If she isn't coming around by next weekend, when we drive down to see her, we'll take her back home with us. Can you hang on until then?"

In the end, he grumbled and gave in. He always gave in when Karla did the asking.

After hanging up the phone, he walked wearily to the door. Cupping his palm round his neck, he looked outside. A light was burning at the guest house. So. She was still up, too. He rubbed a hand roughly over his bleary eyes and, for a brief, shadowy moment, thought he saw her pace by the window. With a deep, slow breath, he turned away.

When he finally hit the sheets, it was with her haunted eyes on his mind. And with the taste of her on his tongue. The feel of her in his arms.

Her scent still filled his senses. She'd been a sweetly exotic blend of honey and silk and wild Texas sage. And salt, he added with a guilt-ridden sigh. She'd tasted of salt from the tears she hated herself for shedding and that he felt like a heel for bringing on.

Hell. He might not have taken Sara Stewart to her

bed tonight, but she sure as hell had managed to find her way into his.

Sara glanced at the clock on the wall, then drummed her fingers nervously against her coffee cup. It was 8:07 a.m. Exactly one minute later than the last time she'd looked. She knew where Lambert would be this time of the morning. She knew there was nothing for it but to face him.

In the week she'd been at Blue Sky, she'd more or less figured out the routine. At seven every morning, Tucker's sister-in-law, Lana, fixed breakfast at the ranch house for anyone who wanted to eat. By that time, Tucker and his brother, Tag, had already done morning chores and started working the horses. After a quick sit-down and a little horseplay with Cody, both went right back to the barns to work until dusk. Much as she wanted to wait until evening to face him, she knew she had to get this over with.

Short on sleep, long on regret, she drained the last of her coffee, rose from the table and tucked her yellow tank top into her jeans. Tugging on her boots and pulling herself together, she headed resolutely out the door. A rolling nausea stopped her before she got through the archway, when she thought of the way she'd thrown herself at the no-good cowboy last night.

She'd stripped for him, for God's sake. She'd all but begged him to take her to bed. Worst of all, she'd let him see how vulnerable she really was.

"Nice work, Stewart," she muttered under her

breath. "Puts the phrase *getting caught with your pants down* in a whole new light."

Her stomach rolled again. She didn't admit to many weaknesses. That Lambert had seen her in the grip of a monster one made her sick with self-loathing.

"There's one thing about it, kiddo," she acknowledged with false brightness, "at least when you screw up, you have the pleasure of knowing that nobody does it better. Queen of the screwups, that's you. High priestess of the royal foul-ups. And champion staller," she added, admitting that this little bit of wordplay was just another ploy to postpone the inevitable.

Nobody could say she didn't own up to her mistakes. With that in mind, she drew a deep breath and walked across the courtyard. Lambert might have been a reluctant knight errant, she had to admit that, but tarnished armor and all, he'd saved her sorry hide last night. Whatever his reasons, she owed him for that; she was a woman who settled her debts.

Though part of her still wanted to hate him for the humiliation, a bigger part thanked God he'd scraped up enough integrity to walk away from her.

Grateful for the dark glasses that covered her eyes and the shadows beneath them, she forced herself to keep walking. The Texas soil dusted her boots with each step. The summer sun, already hot and high, beat down like a furnace on her actively pounding head.

She felt like one big, throbbing nerve. Even without a hangover, this confrontation with Lambert wouldn't have been easy. Facing a lynch mob would have been less painful than doing this with one. To add to her misery, every muscle in her body tightened like a noose knot when she walked into the horse barn and spotted him.

He was standing outside a box stall on the other side of the sawdust-covered floor of the central alley, bridling one of the horses. When he heard her, he glanced her way. After giving her a pensive, assessing once-over from beneath half-lowered lashes, he went back to what he was doing.

From the corner of her eye, she saw Tag bolt out of the tack room, a saddle hefted over his shoulder. When he saw her, he stopped dead in his tracks. With a wary glance from her to Tucker, he very discreetly turned on his worn boot heel and headed back where he'd come from.

Great, she thought. Just great. At least she didn't have to wonder anymore if Tag and Lana knew what had happened last night. It had been a long shot, anyway. The Lord had seen fit to bless her with a great set of pipes. Her threats and screams had probably carried all the way to San Antonio.

Dragging in a bracing breath, she walked the fifty yards in grim silence. Stopping beside the stall, she watched Tucker work a flashy little bay gelding's forelock through the bridle.

When he neither acknowledged nor seemed to notice her presence, she tucked her hands into the hip pockets of her jeans and cleared her throat.

When he still didn't bother to look her way, she lifted her chin and tried not to sound miffed.

"I came to apologize, Lambert."

The only sign he gave that he'd heard her was a slight pause of his hands before he finished buckling the strap beneath the gelding's jaw.

"I was out of line last night," she continued, determined to tough it out. "I'm sorry I put you in an uncomfortable position."

Without ever looking her way, he ran an assessing hand along the colt's withers. "Yeah, well, I figure we've both got a few things to be sorry about."

She closed her eyes and let out a deep breath. If he sensed her relief that it was over, or how hard it had been for her to face him in stark, harsh daylight, he didn't let on.

He could have thrown what she'd done back in her face. In fact, she'd expected him to. But for some reason, he'd chosen not to. Just as he'd chosen not to take her up on her offer last night. On both counts she was grateful. On both counts she was surprised.

More than that, in that moment she thought it might actually be possible to like him for what he'd done. But only a little, she warned herself. Tucker Lambert hadn't gotten his reputation out of a box of cereal. He'd earned it with his fast-and-loose life-style and his don't-give-a-damn ways.

He was a demon in blue denim, a bad seed, she reminded herself as she looked his long, lean frame up and down. Dressed in blue chambray and faded jeans, a light layer of Texas dust coating his leather chaps, he looked too gorgeous for his own good. It was biology, not benevolence, she reminded herself, that flecked his flirty blue eyes with enough dazzle to charm the sun from the Texas sky—or a yes from the woman he chose to turn it on.

Thank God she'd never been a sucker for a killer smile or bought into the line that all a bad man needed was a good woman to straighten him out. Tucker Lambert needed more than a good woman. And whatever he needed, it was a cinch he wasn't going to get it from her. According to Karla, he was beyond redemption. No romanticizing about his uncharacteristic nobility last night was going to make that fact go away.

But she still owed him, and now that the lines of communication were open, all the words she should have said when Karla and Lance left her at Blue Sky tumbled out in one big, massive breath.

"Look," she began, determined to make things right, "I know the way the wind blows. I know Karla and Lance sprung me on you and for some reason they've got you up against the wall on this one so you had to let me stay. You don't want me here. I appreciate that. I don't even blame you. I wouldn't want me here, either."

She paused for a deep breath. "On top of it, I know I haven't exactly been the model houseguest. Lana has gone out of her way to make me feel comfortable, and I've gone out of my way to be distant."

He finally met her eyes. "Seems to me you ought to be saying this to Lana," he said, then turned away again as he hooked a stirrup over the pommel and tightened the cinch strap.

She felt the light sting in his subtle reprimand, but knew she deserved it, and more. He was right. Lana was young and sincere and sweet. As Tag's wife and the only woman in residence on the ranch, Lana took pride in her unofficial role as hostess. She had repeatedly tried to coax Sara to join them for meals. She'd shut off Lana's efforts with stilted no-thank-yous and a depression-induced aloofness. Finally, Lana had quit asking. Sara didn't blame her. But she did blame herself for being so distant. From the beginning she'd felt guilt over that.

"I intend to tell her," she said softly. "Just as soon as I speak my piece to you."

She drew another fortifying breath. "I know you're caught in the cross fire here. That never should have happened, since the plan was to let me drop out of the real world for a while."

He cast her a considering look that gave her the courage to continue.

"Lucky you," she said, with a grim smile. "You just happened to be the drop-off point. For what it's worth, I appreciate that you're putting up with me. And if it makes you feel any better, I could cheerfully strangle Karla and Lance for putting us both in this position.

"It's not fair to you. I never intended to drag you into my problems. I never intended to drag *anybody* into my problems. I don't like it much—this notion that my friends feel I need their help. I like it even less that I added insult to injury with that..." She paused, not wanting to put it into words, but knowing she had to. "That stunt I pulled last night."

She swallowed hard as the shame momentarily out-distanced her resolve. She looked away, closed her eyes and collected herself.

"You hadn't bargained for that," she said, making herself meet his eyes again. "You haven't bargained for any of this. And you shouldn't have to. You weren't supposed to be any more than a distant spectator in my little…" Again, she hesitated, then made herself continue. "In my little breakdown—or whatever the hell it is that's happening to me."

Her breath stalled under the crushing weight of that statement, and she realized that she was shaking. She'd just voiced a concern she'd only last night given up avoiding. With the help of her friend Jack Daniel—or, when the bottle ran dry, too many cool six-packs—she'd managed to deny that she wasn't coping any more.

The brutal reality that she'd just admitted to that ugly little truth aloud—and to Lambert, of all people—sent a chill through her blood that even the heat of this scorching summer day couldn't temper. With the chill, came the fear. She really didn't know what was happening to her. It scared her half to death.

She didn't like being afraid. During the long hours of last night, alone and shocked painfully into sobriety by that cold shower and her shame, she'd decided she had to face her fears. She couldn't run away from them anymore.

At the heart of it all, she didn't like the person

she'd become—a woman who would throw herself at a stranger as a substitute for a solution. She didn't like the face she saw in the mirror. It was haunted and haggard, flushed from the abuses she'd inflicted on herself, stressed with guilt, and now with the humiliation of knowing she'd offered herself like used goods in a pathetic effort to combat her sense of failure.

She became aware, suddenly, of the silence. And of the tightness in her chest, and of the tears stinging her eyes.

Lowering her head, she blinked them back—then almost gave in to them again when Lambert's soft and oddly comforting gaze touched hers.

"For a woman who hadn't strung much more than two words back-to-back since you've been here," he said, flipping the stirrup down then regarding her again over his extended arm, "you sure as hell figured out how to put them all together."

A slight wry grin tilted one corner of his mouth as he smoothed an assessing hand over the gelding's hip, then made a final adjustment on the bit.

She just looked at him as the urge to smile worked at tipping up one corner of her mouth.

So, she was supposed to think he figured that last night's performance and her soul-spilling speech were no big deal, she thought, measuring his words. At least he was trying to convince her it wasn't a big deal. It was a nice thing for him to do. From all she'd been told, it was totally out of character. Just as he'd ducked out of character when he walked away from her last night.

She was beginning to wonder if maybe there was more to Tucker Lambert than his full-of-hell grin and take-no-prisoners reputation suggested. After all, the only thing she really knew about him was what Karla had told her. And Karla had told her to keep her distance.

But for the first time in longer than she could remember, she felt a true smile coming on, over his generosity—and over the pleasant prospect that Tucker Lambert might just be more than met the eye.

"Yeah, well," she said, taking the olive branch he'd offered, trying to cover her embarrassment over baring her soul with a flipness she didn't really feel. "This station is back on the air. I'm talking again, Lambert, so be warned that your reprieve is over."

He looked her in the eye then. The punch that look packed was as explosive as his next words. "Does that mean *your* reprieve has finally begun?"

She sobered abruptly. He wasn't referring to the fact that she'd broken her silence. And while he might not know the full extent of what he was asking, she did. *Are you finished beating yourself up over things you can't control? Are you through blaming yourself for the sins of a society run amok? Are you ready to face the truth of your life and deal with the downside? Are you ready to go back to the job you were trained to do?*

The questions still scared her. She still didn't know the answers. She only knew she didn't like where she'd been heading to find them...or to avoid finding them. While she didn't intend to retrace the path she'd been following, she still didn't know what direction she needed to take to work this through. Not completely.

"Well, let's put it this way," she said, confirming one decision she had reached last night. She and Jackie D were going to part company. It was the first of many overdue steps toward getting her life back together. "From this point on, your virtue is safe from me. You don't have to worry about getting accosted by moonlight again."

A curious mix of approval and pride softened his eyes before he swung into the saddle. But when he'd settled his weight and looked down on her, his devastating grin, full of mischief and impossible to resist, was back in place. "I knew there was a downside to this."

She couldn't stop the laugh from bubbling out. He was working awfully hard at downplaying what was in all probability the most embarrassing night of her life. She wanted to like him for that reason alone. Right or wrong, she decided to let herself. She'd been dodging her gut instincts for too many years. Once the decision was made, it felt good.

"Lambert," she said, stopping him as he gathered the reins. She wanted to tell him how much she appreciated the effort he'd thrown into taking some of the sting out of this for her. But for all the words she'd spouted earlier, the only one she managed now was a soft "Thanks."

He simply nodded, touched his fingers to his hat brim and rode away.

There was nothing simple about her jumbled thoughts as she stood there and watched him go.

Three

Tucker had felt as mean as a rattler and just as low when he crawled out of the sack at five-thirty that morning. His black mood hadn't eased by eight, when he was saddling his second mount and was getting ready to put the flashy three-year-old through his paces.

Then *she'd* shown up. If she'd hit him with a brick, it couldn't have stunned him more than her apology. Before he recovered, she'd slammed him again with her haunting self-assessment.

For a moment, he'd felt like he'd been cheated. He'd known there would be a confrontation between them. He'd been cruising for a knock-down-drag-out. At the very least, a good yelling match.

He'd been ready to lay down the law: *Stay out of*

my way. Stay out of my life. But with quiet, sincere words she'd cleared the air and shown him a strength he hadn't wanted to give her credit for possessing.

He'd searched her face, probed the brown eyes that couldn't quite meet his, and felt that ache of compassion and kinship he'd sworn he wouldn't let himself feel. The look in her eyes as she faced him had been fragile as glass. It had killed her to come to him. To admit her embarrassment and confront it head-on had been bad enough. To apologize had to have damn near done her in.

He'd felt an unsolicited clutch of pride in her, then damned himself for a fool for even thinking along those lines. As he mounted the bay, he'd had to remind himself that she was nothing to him. Nothing but a pain.

Yet even as he kneed the gelding into a trot and rode away, he'd had to squelch the urge to ride right back to her. To avoid it, he'd worked himself and the colt until they were both in a lather.

Even with the workout, and the ones after that, he hadn't been able to shake the memory of the look in her eyes as they searched his. It had been surprisingly soft and uncomfortably pensive. He knew better than to get caught up in caring about those looks. Caring led to expectation. Expectation led to promises. Both were traps he avoided at all costs.

That was why he should have felt irritation when he caught sight of her on the porch swing in the covered courtyard of the ranch house when he came in for supper. What he felt, instead, was too much warmth as he watched her play with baby Cody. And too damn much pleasure at seeing her there.

She was still dressed in the yellow tank top and those soft, tight jeans that hugged her curves like a possessive lover. She looked comfortable and natural, like she belonged on the dust and sage of a working ranch instead of the concrete streets of the city. Her black roper boots showed a respectable amount of wear and fit in the way a pair of fancy fashion boots never would. For some reason, that pleased him. Even the way she wore the straw Stetson she'd settled over her dark hair had Texas Born and Bred stamped all over it.

And the soft smile lighting her face when she saw him, then the attentive way she lifted Cody into her arms and dropped an impulsive kiss on his golden curls, filled his chest with an ache he couldn't have identified or named.

"Hi," she said, rising from her perch on the swing and settling the pudgy little boy onto her hip.

Tucker stopped and frowned, reaching instinctively to brush a knuckle over Cody's soft cheek. The baby squealed in delight. "Tu-er! Tu-er!"

"Take it easy, you little tank," Sara said with a laugh as Cody bounced wildly in her arms. She shifted him from one hip to the other to get him in a better hold, then grinned up at Tucker. "It would seem that he's glad to see you."

Their gazes locked over Cody's head. It was all Tucker could do not to ask if she was glad to see him, too.

Damn fool. Damn stupid fool.

"I hope you don't mind," she said, a wariness coming back into her eyes when she encountered his scowl. "That I'm here for supper, I mean. After I made my apologies to Lana, she insisted I eat with you tonight."

"That sounds like Lana," he said, because it seemed the safest reply. Much safer than satisfying the unbidden urge to lean down and plant a deep, probing kiss on that sweet, sultry mouth of hers.

"It's all right, then?"

Hell, no, it wasn't all right. He needed distance from her, not proximity. But he kept those thoughts to himself and shrugged. "Suit yourself."

He dodged the wounded look in her eyes, skirted around the jumble of thoughts clouding his head, and walked toward the door.

Maybe it was the need he sensed in her that made him want to reassure her and run from her at the same time. That need was as potent as her scent. It drifted on the air as he walked by her, as exotic as sin, yet as fragile as the yellow roses Lana struggled to bring to bloom despite dry winds and searing heat.

The memory of Sara's mouth against his clutched at his gut. He had a miserable feeling her taste would linger in his mind even after her scent had faded—if it ever did. And the wanting that accompanied them both would niggle like a deep, throbbing bruise.

Lana opened the door from inside, just as he reached for it.

"Hey, Tuck." She smiled in greeting as she wiped

her hands on a dish towel, then shoved a fall of heavy black hair behind her ear.

"Tag'll be up in a couple of minutes," he said, following her gaze toward the barns.

"He'd better be," she said with a mock scowl. "Because I'm about to put supper on the table, and I fried that chicken he's been after me to fix." She switched her attention to Sara and the baby. "And how are you two getting on?"

"We're doing just fine, aren't we, big guy?" Sara gave Cody a swift hug, then pressed her cheek to the top of his head when he cuddled against her.

The combination of that instinctive maternal gesture and the sight of the wet spot on her knit top, low on her breast, where the teething two-year-old had drooled, tugged at his chest in a slow, hard pull. Emotions he couldn't catalog, wants he couldn't name, tangled with regrets he hadn't known he harbored and didn't want to admit, confusing the hell out of him as he watched her holding his brother's child.

He tore his gaze away, only to collide with her brown eyes. Softly searching, curiously concerned, she met his eyes for the briefest of moments before Lana's voice jerked him back to the present.

"You have no idea what a help it was having you watch him while I got supper ready," Lana was saying to Sara. "I'd forgotten what it was like not to have him underfoot. Isn't that right, sugar?"

Cody reached for his mother when he heard her voice. Lana enfolded the baby's outstretched hands in her own and nuzzled her face in the curve of his double chins. "You stay with Aunt Sara just a little while longer, okay, baby?"

Tucker's frown deepened and landed on Sara. *Aunt Sara?*

She just shrugged and gave him a helpless grin.

With a snort, he stalked on into the house to clean up. And sort out. And think through.

This was getting sticky. He hit the shower cursing the day he'd set eyes on Sara Stewart. He didn't like what was happening here. It wasn't just the ease with which she had won Lana's confidence. It was more the sense that she seemed to have entrusted that same kind of confidence to him. He wasn't comfortable with it. Or with the things she made him feel.

Or with the look in her eyes this morning and again tonight when she'd first spotted him, he added grimly. He'd seen that look too many times over the years not to recognize it for what it was. Interest. Physical and emotional. Her curiosity was piqued. Her expectations were heightened. *Is there more to the man than the face and body? Is there substance and strength and something worth finding inside?*

Honey, he thought darkly, the answers would disappoint you.

Twisting off the spray, he reached for a towel. He'd known from the outset that she was trouble. What he hadn't known was that he'd feel this attraction toward her—or this sense of responsibility. He didn't need Sara Stewart to add to the list of people who depended on him.

He didn't want to be responsible for her. It was a

given that if she cast her lot with him, he'd let her down. When it came to women, he always did. That was one of the reasons he'd done his damnedest to keep his distance. But now that he'd looked into Sara Stewart's eyes, he had another reason. The bottom line was, if he let himself, he could care about her.

He already cared enough that he didn't want to hurt her—and enough that he didn't want her to find him out. Just as she was running from a life she could no longer cope with, he was dodging his own demons— demons that constantly reminded him he couldn't give any more to a relationship than good sex and bad goodbyes.

He wasn't proud of it. He wasn't pleased by it, either. It was just a fact. He couldn't commit. Couldn't be depended on. It wasn't even his fault. It was a matter of blood—a legacy from his father.

The genetic accident of good looks and a winning grin were all John Lambert had ever given him. Hard times and excuses were all his father had ever given Tucker's mother. Tucker had watched it break her, then finally kill her.

He lived with the memory of his mother's death and the knowledge that he was just like his old man. He looked like him. He charmed like him. He had the same capacity for using it all to his advantage. The knowledge ate at him like acid.

He'd found out at an early age that he had the same power over women as John Lambert, and he'd sworn he would never be responsible for causing the kind of pain his father had caused his mother.

That was why he kept his involvements with women fast and loose. No strings. No strain. No misunderstandings that permanence was part of the plan. If they didn't understand the rules up front, they didn't play the game. Not with him.

Miz Sara Stewart didn't yet know the rules. She wasn't a player in his kind of game. She was a forever kind of woman. In spite of her coming on to him last night, he knew that one-night stands weren't a regular part of her agenda.

He smiled grimly. In spite of what had happened between them, she thought he was a nice guy. He could see it in her smile. Hear it in her voice.

He pulled on clean jeans, and with grim determination made up his mind. If she kept giving him those soft, slow looks and those shy, sexy smiles, he was going to have to set her straight.

"Thanks," Tucker mumbled, but didn't look up, when Sara passed him the basket of rolls.

"You're welcome," she replied, then caught herself before she asked him what was wrong. For some reason, she was making him nervous. The man was as skittish as a calf at branding time. He thought he was hiding it. He thought he was handling it. He was wrong. Judging from the puzzled looks passing between Lana and Tag, they were at a loss as to what was bothering him, too.

"So, big bro," Tag said, tearing a warm bun in half and slathering it with butter, "is that little roan gonna be ready for Galveston?"

"She's coming along," Tucker said, and dived into his meal again.

Sara looked from Tucker to his younger brother and understood the reason for the adoring glances that Lana cast her husband's way. Tag was almost a carbon copy of Tucker. He was muscled yet lean, with the same burnished-gold hair, the same tight cowboy butt, and that trademark Lambert smile that could charm a nun out of her habit and into a teddy. Tag might be young—barely into his twenties, she'd guess—but in spite of his boyish teasing and his sometimes macho posturing for Lana, his manner conveyed an underlying maturity and sense of responsibility beyond his years.

It was there in Tucker, too. Not in words so much as in action. He worked hard. They both did. She'd gotten the feeling in the few days she'd been here that both men were driven to succeed by something more far-reaching than paying the bills or getting rich. It was as if they had something to prove. Who they needed to prove it to was anyone's guess.

Tag obviously didn't have to prove anything to Lana. She was a dark-eyed beauty, young and in love and as natural a mother as Sara had ever seen. If she didn't miss her guess, Lana was also in the bloom of the first few months of another pregnancy.

"Saw Sam Commins in town the other day," Tag offered, interrupting her thoughts, as he stabbed another piece of chicken from the platter. "Says he'll be out one of these first days to check on his filly."

Tucker snorted. "Let's just hope he has his check-book in his hand when he gets here."

"Mason came through," Lana offered brightly. "Paid in full, plus two months ahead."

"Amazing what placing in the money a couple of times will do to loosen up the green," Tag said, grinning. "That mare of his is one sweet little lady. If she keeps up the pace, she'll do more'n place her next few times out. She'll be finishing in the top two or three. The buzz about her will be just what Blue Sky needs to attract more business."

"And the buzz about Poco when he wins the futurity in Fort Worth this winter will guarantee it keeps coming," Tucker added confidently. "That little stud's going to write our ticket to a long and prosperous future."

Tag tossed his brother an ornery grin. "That little stud's gonna land you and your sorry butt in the dust if you don't keep your mind on your business any better than you did today."

"You let me worry about Poco," Tucker said with a warning glare, and pushed away from the table. "And we'll worry about business tomorrow. I've had as much as I can handle for one day.

"Good supper, Lana," he added as he stood up and chucked Cody under his double chin.

The baby squealed and offered Tucker a bite from his spoonful of mashed potatoes.

"You eat it, little cowpoke," he said, grinning. "If y'all will excuse me, I'm outa here."

He didn't wait for anyone to respond. Judging from

the look Lana and Tag exchanged as he left the room, Sara sensed that his destination was neither a surprise nor a mystery to them.

She wasn't so lucky. The clutch of disappointment that hit her hard and fast was a big surprise. The devastation she felt when he sauntered toward the door without a backward glance was a total mystery.

"Oh-oh," Tag uttered as he watched his brother snag a black Resistol from the rack and head out the door. "The black hat."

"The black hat?" Sara echoed, sensing a significance she wasn't sure she wanted to be privy to.

"His prowling hat," Lana explained, casting a worried glance Tucker's way before she met Tag's scowl. "A heart's gonna get broken tonight," she said with a resigned sigh, and started clearing the table.

A heart's gonna get broken tonight. The words echoed through Sara's mind as she rose in stilted silence to help Lana with the dishes. With concentrated effort, she avoided looking out the window as the sound of a pickup tearing out of the drive infiltrated the evening silence.

Some poor unsuspecting woman was going to feel the heat of Tucker Lambert's passion and the sting of his goodbye. Sara could almost have felt sorry for her—if she didn't already feel sorry for herself.

Sara told herself she had her head back on straight by midnight. At least in regard to Tucker Lambert.

She'd even rationalized her reactions to him and fit them into neat little columns to explain them away.

Curled up in the corner of the overstuffed sofa in her tiny living room, she'd sat in the dark and sorted it all out. He'd been a surprise, was all. A bad boy hiding a good heart. A shock to her system. Lord knew her system was ready to welcome a shock. At least a different kind from the ones she was used to dealing with in ER. The kind that had her dodging grisly reality with the void of numbness. She'd gotten good at feeling nothing. So good she'd crumbled under the strain. She recognized that now.

Laying her head back against the sofa cushions, she worked on forgiving herself. Karla had been right. A little time. A little distance. A lot of soul-searching. That would help her get grounded again. Then she could decide what she was going to do with the rest of her life.

In the meantime, Tucker Lambert's blond good looks and you-don't-know-what-you're-missing-grin had snapped that ironclad grip she'd held on her emotions. He'd simply proved that she wasn't immune to a pretty face and the promise of pleasure. And that she was weary of living in a void. Her responses had been natural and physical.

If she'd been hitting on all four cylinders, she'd have dealt with them, dismissed them, and gone on about her business. She wouldn't have romanticized the way he'd protected her pride and her integrity. And she wouldn't have spent the day convincing herself he might be more than he wanted everyone to see.

Toward evening, though, it had been Lana doing the convincing. This no-account cowboy, who wasn't supposed to be good for anything but grief, walked on water, as far as Lana was concerned. Sara snuggled deeper into the sofa and thought back to their conversation over the supper dishes.

"Tag and I might not be together now if it wasn't for Tucker. Isn't that right, sugar?" Lana had cooed as she leaned over the baby, who was happily banging a spoon against his high-chair tray. "I was three months pregnant, sick as a dog, and living in a dingy one-room walk-up in Dallas. I was too sick to work and existing from week to week on the money Tag sent home from his work on road construction."

Sara had seen the flashback to depression in Lana's eyes as she remembered that time. Sara had felt for her. Lana had been young, pregnant and lonely. Tag had been trying to do his best by her. He'd kept a roof over her head and food in her mouth, but at great cost to their young marriage.

"Tucker took us away from all that and brought us here to Blue Sky. Even before that, though," Lana had continued as she handed a plate to Sara to dry, "Tucker had been the only stable force in Tag's life."

"How so?" she'd asked, unable to stanch the curiosity and the respect she was beginning to feel for Tucker.

"When the boys' mother died, Tag was only fourteen. I didn't know him then, but I guess he went a little wild with grief. Crazy with pain, you know? He'd dropped out of everything that would have been good for him and into everything that was bad. Tucker was only twenty-six himself, but he came back to Dallas and took charge.'' She'd paused and smiled fondly. ''To hear them talk, it was a rocky road for both brothers.''

When she put it all together, Sara knew it was also a measure of Tucker's worth that he'd managed not only to get his renegade teenage brother under control, but also develop the close relationship they had today.

''Where was their father during all this?'' she'd asked, half suspecting what Lana would say.

''They don't talk about him much. From everything I've gathered, he wasn't much of a factor in their lives.''

Unless you consider the fact that he wasn't ever there for them, Sara thought with brooding speculation.

She tucked her feet under her bottom and stared into the darkness. So Tucker hadn't had an easy go of it. So in spite of that, he wasn't a total bad guy. That still didn't account for her preoccupation with him, or the disappointment she felt knowing he was probably with another woman right now.

She had no claim on him. In fact, the notion was ridiculous. Yet she felt a low, dull ache of sadness because of it. Maybe it all came down to loneliness. She'd been alone a long time. On her own. Coping. Existing. She'd always thought that was the way she wanted it. But she was beginning to wonder. If she'd had someone to share the ugly, as well as the good, maybe she wouldn't have gotten into the shape she was in now. Sharing seemed to work for Karla and Lance.

It seemed to work for Tag and Lana, too. Watching them together this past week had started a slow, steady tug on all those yearnings she'd denied for the sake of her career. As young as they were, they were solid in their love. They were beautiful together. Earlier tonight, when they thought they were alone, she'd felt a little like a voyeur, watching them from the darkness of her courtyard. But the scene had been so riveting as they stood outside on their veranda, wrapped in each other's arms, cocooned from the rest of the world, she hadn't been able to tear her gaze away.

Lana's back had rested against Tag's chest, his broad shoulders had cushioned her head. His lean fingers had spread low across her belly, possessive and prideful, as she'd turned her face to his for a deep, thorough kiss. It had been a sweet and sexy pose. Poignant yet erotic. A man loving his woman. A woman loving her man. The special bond they shared because of the baby growing inside her body was the ultimate completion of their love.

Sara's inability to stop herself from watching them brought the stark reality of her solitary existence home—and her thoughts back to Tucker, just as the lights of a vehicle swung into the drive.

Her gaze snapped to the clock. For a man who'd

left with hell-raising on his mind, Tucker was home pretty early, she thought as she heard the motor idle, then die.

"And for a woman who's trying to convince herself that in this life or any other Tucker Lambert is not the man for you, you're a little too pleased by that conclusion, Stewart," she muttered under her breath.

Still, she rose slowly from the sofa and, fighting all the reasons she shouldn't, walked on bare feet to the screen door.

Unlike last night, the sky was overcast, the moon a pleasant memory tucked behind dingy, scudding clouds. Outside the casa, it was dark on dark. Shadow on shadow. And Tucker Lambert was a part of it all.

Her heart stumbled when the driver's door swung open and he eased his long legs slowly to the ground. His silhouette was as black as midnight as he shut the door, then slumped beside the truck, his head bowed, his elbows propped behind him on the side of the pickup's bed. And he didn't move again.

For a full minute, she stood in silence, watching him. Wondering if he was thinking, or sleeping, or just dead drunk. Wondering why she cared.

The screen door creaked as it opened and closed behind her. For a long moment, she stood barefoot on the tile, her arms hugged around her waist, her loose cotton nightgown rustling around her legs in the sweet night breeze.

"You okay?" she finally called out softly. The healer in her, she told herself, made her do it.

No response.

With a glance toward Tag and Lana's casa that confirmed all was dark over there, she stepped out from under the archway and into the dry Texas dust.

"Tucker," she whispered when she reached his side. When he didn't respond, she touched a hand to his shoulder. "Are you all right?"

"Fit," he said, without ever raising his head, "as a freaking fiddle."

He smelled of barroom smoke and stale beer. And cheap perfume.

"Rough night?" she asked dryly around a disappointed trip of her heart.

He tipped his head back and, bleary-eyed, focused on the sky, avoiding her measuring stare. "Not rough enough."

"You're drunk," she stated flatly.

He grunted and brought a hand to his eye. "Not—" he paused, grimacing when he touched it "—drunk enough." Which implied, of course, that he was.

She walked around him to the cab and opened the door. The dome light cast just enough light for her to see the right side of his face and the slight swelling above his eye clearly.

"Well," she said, shutting the door and dousing the light. "I suppose I ought to see the other guy."

He just snorted.

"Come on," she said, half in disgust, half in resignation as it hit home that he was every bit the rounder and the renegade he'd been billed as. "I'll take care of it."

"I don't think I want you takin' care of me."

The hard edge to his voice had her turning back to face him. The belligerence in his glare dared her to back down.

"Tell it to someone who cares what you think," she said, returning his puzzling hostility with the bite of her own.

Telling herself she couldn't care less if he followed her, she left him in the darkness. Yet somehow she knew he'd show. She was waiting for him in the kitchen when he opened the door.

Slow and surly, he stalked into the room, all broad shoulders, narrow hips and heart-kicking sexy scowl.

His gaze raked her body as she stood in bare feet and her cool cotton gown. In the pale glow cast by the light above the stove, his blue eyes glittered, dark and dangerous and full of sexual heat. In a silence interrupted only by the distant ticking of a clock, her heart echoed out her own awareness.

With a grim determination to patch him up and send him home, she motioned him toward a chair. He sat with a bored, beleaguered sigh and tossed his hat on the kitchen table.

"So," she said when she'd satisfied herself that the cut was superficial and the worst he'd get out of it was a small scar, "is this a Wednesday-night ritual?"

He flinched when she dabbed a soapy gauze pad on the cut to clean it. "Used to be," he grumbled, then added, as if it disgusted him, "Guess I'm out of practice."

For some reason, that small, telling admission pleased her. Not, she tried to convince herself, that she cared what he did or didn't do with his nights.

"Well, lucky for you the guy who hit you didn't pack much of a punch."

He was silent for a long moment before he spoke. When he did, his voice was as hard as his eyes. "The *guy's* name was Rita," he said, clearly intending to shock her, as he watched her face, gauging her reaction. "And it wasn't a punch. It was a miscalculation. Took a hell of a hit on the headboard of her bed."

A lump that was more than disappointment and too much like pain dropped like a stone to her stomach. The hand that tended his wound stilled, then went back to work, a little too vigorously, as she tried to deal with emotions she shouldn't be feeling. Not for him.

"Ouch. Woman, leave some skin."

She took a small measure of satisfaction in his pain. Realizing how perverse that was, she dropped her hand.

"Just...just let me put a dressing on it and you can go home to bed."

Bed. Swallowing hard, she tried to block the picture of Rita with the bad perfume and Tucker stretched out across one. She reached for the box of tape.

"Lose the wounded look, darlin'."

Her head snapped around at the dangerous edge in his voice. The night grew agonizingly quiet as their gazes locked under the pale kitchen light.

"And don't give me that mystified stare." His expression was cold and mean and nasty. "You're messing with the wrong man here. You're disappointed, right? You thought ol' Tuck might not be the big bad hombre you'd heard he was. You thought maybe, just maybe, I might be worth a deeper look."

She closed her eyes and swallowed hard, humiliated, hurt and exposed. He was right. As right as she was wrong for thinking those things about him.

"Well, what you see is what you get, darlin'. I'm as bad as they say I am. Maybe worse. Hell. I don't even know Rita's last name. I only know she had a nice ass and great set of—"

"You've made your point, Lambert," she said, cutting him off and stuffing adhesive and gauze back into the first-aid kit.

"Have I?" In a lightning move, he snagged her arm and pulled her onto his lap. His fingers clamped round her wrist in a bruising grip. "Have you really gotten the message?"

Ignoring her struggling attempt to escape him, he wrapped his arms around her and dragged her roughly against him.

"I'm a user, little girl," he growled, snagging a handful of her hair in his fist and pulling her mouth within an inch of his. "You give me the chance, I'll use you up. Or is that what you want?"

She didn't know what she wanted. But it wasn't

this. She swallowed hard. "No," she whispered. "That's not what I want."

He let out a tired, heavy sigh. "Then you'd better run, little Miz Sara," he murmured as he loosened his grip on her hair and, with the pressure of his hand on her jaw, tipped her head so that her eyes were on a level with his. "You'd better run far and you'd better run fast."

His callused fingers stroked her cheek. His beckoning blue eyes were soft and searching and laced with something that looked suspiciously like regret. "Because if you stay round me much longer, there's not going to be anything left of you to take back to Dallas."

After a long, searching look, he released her and slumped back in the chair. "Now git."

Four

If Sara had been smart, she would have run. She would have scrambled off his lap and out of the kitchen and locked the bedroom door behind her. But she couldn't seem to move. She just sat there, her hands poised on his broad shoulders, her heart pumping, her head clouded with confusion.

With a slow shake of his head, Tucker closed his eyes, then drew a deep, ragged breath. "Don't have the smarts God gave a rock, do you?" he concluded wearily. "Not when it comes to taking care of yourself."

It was then that things started coming together in Sara's mind—and in her heart. Something wasn't ringing true here. He was telling her to go, but his touch, his tone of voice, his eyes, were all at odds with his words. He wanted her to stay. And no matter how ugly a picture he'd painted of himself, his blue eyes begged her not to believe it.

It came to her then that she wasn't the only one hurting. He was hurting, too, covering his own pain even as he tried to harden himself against hers. A memory from last night—the moment before he'd first kissed her—came back with crystal clarity.

She'd sensed a vulnerability in him then. She sensed it again now. In his voice, in his words, in the soulful loneliness of his tortured blue gaze.

"What I don't have," she began, as a sure, creeping conviction began to take root, "is a take on what this grand gesture of warning is all about."

He looked momentarily taken aback before he tried to hide it behind a smile as dark as it was wicked.

"Trust me, darlin'. This is no grand gesture. It's a warning. Simple and true. But I can see it's going to take some convincing to make you see the light. I didn't take advantage last night, Miz Sara Sunshine, because I like my women fully revved when we cross that finish line. You weren't racing on a full tank." His smile twisted nastily.

"But that's not the case tonight, is it? You know exactly what's going to happen if you don't get the hell away from me. And so help me, it won't be me putting on the skids tonight. Tonight, you're the only one who can do the saving."

As if to prove his point, he tightened his hands on her hips, blatantly kneading as his gaze dropped from her face to boldly stare at her breasts and the dark shadows of her nipples, pressing against the thin cotton of her low cut nightgown.

She should have felt insulted. He'd intended her to. She should have been offended. He'd planned on that, too. Instead, she felt a tingling longing and a melting heat when he raised a dark, callused hand and caressed her through the lightweight fabric.

On its heels came a warming tenderness and rush of emotion made sweeter by a sense of rightness as strong as any she'd ever known. And when he lowered his head to her breast and nuzzled her through the soft, sheer cotton, she sucked in her breath, welcoming the hot, intimate contact.

"Run, darlin'," he murmured—half warning, half plea—as he brushed his lips across her erect nipple.

She lowered her mouth to his golden hair. "You weren't with another woman tonight," she whispered.

He went very still. When he raised his face to hers, the look in his eyes confirmed her suspicion and her next statement as fact. "You aren't even drunk," she continued, daring him to deny what her heart told her was true. "You're stone-cold sober."

She lowered her hands to his chest, needing to feel his heat and experience his reaction. His heart beat like thunder beneath her hands, an affirmation of his lie, giving her the courage to press him.

"Why did you lie to me, Tucker?"

He didn't answer. He didn't have to. The look on his face told her why. He'd lied to protect her. To protect her from him.

"What kind of big, bad user warns his target

away?'' she asked gently, then saw, too clearly, his difficulty in dealing with the implications of her accusation.

For some reason, this man who had taken care of his orphaned brother and was committed to the needs of his family, had painted himself as the loser who wasn't entitled to any commitments of his own.

It finally came to her as she searched his eyes, eyes that were blue and aching with loneliness, why he was warning her off. He was afraid. That was it in a gold-plated nutshell. Tucker Lambert, a self-professed heartbreak kid, was afraid of heartbreak himself.

''Why, Tucker?'' she whispered, as the bleakness in his eyes supported her conclusion and made her own heart ache for him. ''Why did you lie?''

Long after he'd grunted something to the effect that she didn't know what she was talking about, long after he'd set her forcefully off his lap and stalked out the kitchen door, she stared after him.

Long after he'd disappeared into the shadows of the night, she wondered if she'd done the right thing when she let him go.

''What made you afraid, Tucker?'' Her question bounced off the walls of the empty room. ''What's got you running away?''

She knew all about running. She knew how lonely it was. Yet as she stood in the dark, thinking of him, she felt less alone than she had in a long, long time. The knowledge that he, too, had dragons to slay downscaled the scope of her own problems to a more manageable level. The need that he tried so hard to conceal tugged at strings in her heart that had been out of tune for a very long time.

The world was full of wounded people. Who'd have thought that one of them would come wrapped in a package so flashy and flirty that it hid all the wreckage within? Who would have thought, she wondered, crawling into her empty bed, that Tucker Lambert had a soul as scarred as her own?

The first play a cutting horse made on a calf was a thrill Tucker had never quite managed to put into words. It was one of the things that had attracted him to cutting in the first place, that and a love for horses that had hooked him as a kid and hung tight. A friend had once described the sensation of riding a cutter as just like jumping out of a two-story building with a suitcase between your legs.

Tucker supposed that was as close to a description as any. It was all speed and propulsion rocketing you and the horse into one wild jerk-and-glide ride that, in a competition, was over in two and a half minutes. In business, however, it was a daily workout if you wanted to stay on the cutting edge.

Mounting up, settling in, hanging on. It was his life. He was in it for the money, sure, but he was addicted to the sport, too. It had never failed to suck him in, then grab all his physical and mental attention into one focused, consuming sphere of concentration.

Until she'd come along.

Damn the woman. He could still see her eyes searching his last night. Still hear her voice, and the question that was less accusation than it was concern. *"Why did you lie to me, Tucker?"*

How did you know? he'd wanted to shout as he stomped out of her kitchen. *Why do you care? Why don't you just accept that it's the way I am?*

And why, for God's sake, when he was trying his damnedest to warn her away, didn't she have sense enough to run like hell in the opposite direction? Instead, he was the one who'd run, right out her back door and to his empty bed.

He settled deeper into the saddle, trying to concentrate on Poco's moves, willing himself to focus on the calf.

All he saw was Sara Stewart, in her soft, sheer nightie, and her big brown eyes.

The woman looked too deep to suit him. She expected too much. She thought there was more to him than was actually there. Most women knew better. They got a fix on him the first time they sized him up. Good looks, good time, good-bye. That was all there was to Tucker Lambert. They accepted that and didn't ask for more.

She was asking, though. She had expectations he'd fought all his life not to fulfill. She was asking him to prove to her that he was less instead of more. The worst of it was, she made him want to give up the fight.

He swore under his breath. The weekend couldn't come soon enough to suit him. When Karla and Lance came to check on her, he'd send her, none too politely, on her way. Close the chapter. End the book.

In the meantime, he wasn't worth spit.

He climbed reluctantly out of the saddle. "Sorry, ol' buddy. My head's not in the game today.

"Yeah," he said, commiserating, when Poco snorted and pawed the ground with restless, unleashed energy. He knew how the young stallion felt. His blood was running hot and fast, and he was ready for action. Tucker had just let him down. But he'd brought this little stud too far to lose in one morning all the ground he'd gained. As muzzy-headed as he was today, that was exactly what would happen. The futurity was six months away, and he didn't want to take any chances with the three-year-old.

"Problem, bro?"

Tucker avoided his brother's measuring gaze as he led the stud past him toward the barn. "Gettin' old," he grumbled evasively.

Tag's snort told Tucker he wasn't buying it.

Tucker's answering scowl told Tag not to push it. He let out a breath of relief, when, after a long, puzzled look, Tag rode Mason's mare into the holding pen to warm her up.

"Let me get him stalled, then I'll hold the cuts for you," Tucker said, knowing that the prospect of putting the mare through her paces would divert Tag's attention.

Tag had been itching to get a shot at the flashy black ever since they'd unloaded her from Jud Mason's trailer this spring. It was usually Tag's job to hold the calf within working range after Tucker had cut it from the herd.

"You're the boss," Tag said, unable to conceal his excitement as he leaned down to unlatch the gate and ride the mare into the pen with the herd of calves. "But it's not going to be easy shorthanded."

"I think we can handle it."

Tag was right, though; it wasn't easy. Lana had often filled in as a second hand when they were between wranglers. She was a good rider, and level-headed—and she enjoyed the action. But since she'd become pregnant, Tag wouldn't let her within petting distance of a horse, let alone in a saddle. Unfortunately, their last hired hand hadn't worked out—spent his pay in the local roadhouse and his mornings hung over. They'd had to let him go last week, and they were still waiting for their help-wanted ad to be answered.

Tag's first cut into the herd led to frustration for both horse and rider when Tucker, without another hand, couldn't hold the calf in a range close enough for the mare to work effectively.

Tucker was about to give it up when he noticed Sara, her elbows propped on the top fence rail, her expression watchful. She was dressed in faded denim again, along with her worn boots and the straw Stetson that was both work-worthy and sexy.

"I can help," she offered when Tucker looked her way.

He snorted, not about to let the work he'd thrown into avoiding her since last night go down the tubes. "I don't think so."

"No. Really. I can. I used to hold for my daddy when I was a kid."

"Your daddy?"

"Paul Stewart. He's been big in—"

"I know who he is," Tucker said, cutting her off, his voice going as cold as a winter wind.

His heart suddenly felt as heavy as stone in his chest. Anyone who knew anything about the National Cutting Horse Association knew that Paul Stewart wasn't just big in cutting, he was the biggest. Tucker knew Paul Stewart on a more personal note, though, a note that had soured over time and never quite played itself out.

He should have known. He should have put it together that Sara was from *that* Stewart family.

"Daddy won the open futurity in '88 and '89. And back in '80, he let me hold for him in the semifinals. Thought I was just about the biggest cat on the fence that day," she said with a smile. "I was fourteen. And I was in hog heaven."

And I was eighteen, Tucker remembered, thinking back to that summer when he'd worked on her daddy's ranch. He'd known Stewart had a daughter. Might even have caught a glimpse of her now and again from afar. Might even have made a play for her, if she'd been older—and if he hadn't already been making time.

A wave of disgust swamped him, a sickening sense of self-assessment that even sixteen years later he had difficulty forgiving as youthful indiscretion, raging hormones and the practiced manipulations of a woman well versed in the art of seduction.

"So how 'bout it?" Tag's question dragged him back to a moment that was as ironic as fate was twisted. If he'd ever thought, even for a moment, that he could look for something more than a temporary involvement with Sara, that thought had just been trampled into the dry Texas dust.

Paul Stewart's daughter. Just hearing the name was enough to toughen his resolve to keep away from her. No amount of temptation—whether thinking of her or facing her head-on—could bend his will to stay away from her now.

He scowled at her beneath the brim of his hat. "How long since you rode?"

If she noticed the change from moody reluctance to firm resolve, she didn't show it. She grinned at him. "Too long. And the longer I watch you two, the more I realize how much I miss it."

"Third stall, south side of the alley," he said, after a long moment. "Jezibel. She's a sweet little mare with a soft mouth and a nice disposition, so go easy on her. You know where the tack room is."

She gave him a slow, excited smile, backed a step away from the paddock fence then turned and headed for the barn at a trot.

"I'll go help her saddle up," Tag offered, riding toward the gate.

Tucker stopped him with a shake of his head. "She'll do it. If she can't handle it, I don't want her out here with these horses. We're getting paid a lot

of money to give some high-priced horseflesh profes-
sional training. We can't afford to have anyone in
here who doesn't know what they're doing.''

Just like he couldn't afford to wallow in regrets
about what might have been. Of what never should
have been in the first place.

Now that he knew she was Paul Stewart's daughter,
Sara was so far off-limits that she could have been in
another country, for all he cared.

When she joined them riding Jezibel, however, he
couldn't help but admit appreciatively that Miz Stewart knew what she was about. She was a natural rider.
Had a good seat and soft hands. And she hadn't been
blowing smoke. She knew how to hold a calf.

She was tougher than she looked, too. Holding was
a tiresome, sometimes boring job. A lot of sitting and
watching, and then quick reaction was called for. She
did it well. It didn't take long to see why her daddy
had trusted her in an event as prestigious as the futurity.

Unfortunately, it took even less time for him to
realize that he didn't have as much resolve as he
thought. Not where she was concerned.

He'd been determined not to feel anything toward
her. Not longing, not regret. Just indifference. But by
the time the day was over and she'd ridden through
the rest of the workouts, he'd gained a grudging admiration, not only for her riding ability, but for her
grit, too. She'd hung tight in the saddle. Hadn't com-
plained about a thing. Not the heat, not the pace, not

even the dust that covered her clothes and mixed with perspiration to track down her face.

At the end of the day's workout, when he and Tag had broken out a couple of longnecks from the fridge in the barn and offered one to her, he'd upgraded admiration to respect. She'd turned the ice-cold beer down in favor of a can of soda.

When the lady said no more, it seemed that she meant it.

It was more than he could say for himself. Against his will, he watched her as she sprawled on a hay bale in the alley of the barn outside the office. She sagged against the wall, her hat beside her, her hair finger-raked away from a face flushed with heat and fatigue and streaked with sweat and dirt. And he thought she was just about the prettiest thing he'd ·ever seen.

Tag drained his bottle, stretched hugely, then thumbed back his hat. "That's a wrap for me, kids. I'm heading for the shower."

"We're right behind you," Tucker said, but stood where he was, the cold bottle clasped loosely in his hand as he leaned a shoulder against the wall and told himself he could control this until Karla and Lance got her out of his hair.

"Catch you at the supper table, then," Tag said as he headed for the house. "Thanks, cowboy," he added, stopping to toss Sara a quick, approving grin. "Ya done good."

She beamed up at him as if he'd just given her the ultimate compliment. "You're very welcome."

She was still smiling as she watched Tag go. Then she turned her dark eyes on Tucker.

And he was still scowling, wondering what it was about her that wouldn't let him look past her the way he did every other woman like her whose path he crossed. He dismissed her kind without a second look. They were the kind who wanted forever. The kind he didn't make the mistake of giving even the time of day. And she, of all the women in the world, was the one he couldn't have had even if he decided to change his tune.

He was making mistakes with this little cowgirl. He was letting those soft brown eyes get to him. Letting her expectations weigh heavy on his mind. Letting his own wants outdistance the reality of his past.

He touched his fingers absently to the cut above his swollen eye. Hell, because of her, he'd even felt the sting of Rita's anger when he turned down her offer for a quick tumble and a mutually satisfying night.

Only nothing seemed satisfying in that area anymore. Nothing but the prospect of Sara Stewart between his sheets, of him between her thighs. And he wasn't about to let that happen. No way. Once would never be enough with her. Once was all he had in him by way of commitment. Not to mention that once she found out about him, it would be all over, anyway.

"Is it bothering you?" he heard her ask, then realized he was absently rubbing the bandage as he watched her.

She was talking about the cut. And no—it wasn't bothering him, not the way she thought. She was bothering him. He had to figure out what to do about it.

"It's fine," he said brusquely. "And you're beat. Go clean up, then come to supper."

"Yes, boss," she shot back with an ornery grin.

"I didn't mean—"

"To be giving orders?" she asked. "I know. It's okay. I am beat, but you know what? I can't remember when I enjoyed a workout more."

"Yeah, well—" he couldn't quell the admiration "—like Tag said, you're a real cowboy."

She rose and stretched the kinks out, laughing through a grimace as she did. "I bet I smell like one, too. See you at supper." She stopped halfway to the barn door. "Can I come back and play again tomorrow?"

He shouldn't let her. He should say no, if for no other reason than to bank on the old out of sight, out of mind adage helping him make it through the day. But she looked so hopeful and so thoroughly guileless as she stood waiting for his reply that he didn't have it in him to say no.

"We'll see," he said instead. "You're going to have a few ticked-off muscles, not to mention a bruised butt, when you bail out of bed in the morning. You may not be up to it."

"Oh, I'll be up to it," she assured him, and turned around, giving him a view of her saucy little bottom in those tight, worn jeans. A bottom he'd held in his palms not two nights ago. A bottom that had pressed against him as he tugged her onto his lap in her kitchen last night.

He stood there, getting hard just thinking about it. About how sweetly her soft pink cheeks had filled his palms. About how silky her skin had felt beneath his callused hands.

About how much he wanted to take that little cowboy to his bed and into his heart and let her convince him he was worth her time.

He looked away, then pitched the empty longneck toward the recycling barrel.

Paul Stewart's daughter, he thought with a shake of his head as he headed up to the house, a safe distance behind her. Damned if life wasn't just one swift kick in the ass.

When Karla and Lance pulled into the drive at Blue Sky two days later, they looked first at the trio in the cutting corral, then at each other.

"Interesting," Lance said, easing his long legs out of the luxury compact and watching his wife's face as she stepped out the other side.

"Very," she agreed, then walked with Lance toward the corral.

They waved at the riders working the horses, but kept silent, taking as much pleasure in watching the action as they did in this surprising turn of events.

"Could it be they've made some sort of peace?" Lance asked with a pensive grin.

"I don't know," Karla said, after a long, appraising look at Sara, who sat astride a buckskin mare, holding

a calf with Tag as Tucker worked his sorrel stallion.
"But she looks wonderful."

"And he looks like he chewed horseshoes for
breakfast," Lance added speculatively as Tucker let
the calf go and headed, along with Tag and Sara, in
their direction.

Sara flashed a quick, nervous smile at Lance before
swinging her gaze, somewhat warily, to meet Karla's.
"Hey, you," she said finally.

Karla visibly relaxed and returned her tentative
smile. "Hey, yourself."

The unasked questions hovered in Karla's eyes.
*"How are you? I've been worried about you. Are you
still angry with me for interfering?"*

"We didn't mean to interrupt anything," Lance
said into a silence filled with long looks and uncomfortable shifting. "Go ahead and finish your workout."

"We just did," Tucker said, grim-faced, as he
swung out of the saddle.

"Looks like you've got yourself a new wrangler
here," Lance added, with an approving nod toward
Sara.

"Just filling in," she said, for some reason not
wanting Karla or Lance to read more into the situation
than there was. Not that there was more to the situation, she reminded herself…nothing more than a
hundred undercurrents that had been tugging at both
her sexuality and her heart for the past few days.

"Seems the least I could do," she added, with a
pointed stare at her friends that was meant to remind

them that she hadn't forgotten they'd dumped her here.

"She's as savvy as an old pro," Tag put in, in a not-so-subtle attempt to diffuse the tension. "Ain't that right, bro?"

Tucker just glared. "I need to talk to you, Griffin." He turned toward the barn, his expectation that Lance would follow as explicit as if he'd barked an order.

"Well," Tag said brightly as he watched the two men walk away, "If you ladies'll excuse me, I'll just go see if those are chocolate chip cookies I've been smelling all morning. Lana's cookies are the best this side of Waco."

In silence, the two women watched him go.

"You look good, Sara," Karla said after a long moment.

"I'm getting there," she said, realizing as she did that it was the first time she'd admitted to her friend that she'd been in trouble. "And no—I'm not mad anymore," she added, with a crooked grin that changed in a thought to a grimace. "Just embarrassed."

"No need." Karla's eyes were soft. "You needed a little rest, that's all."

"I needed a swift kick," Sara said with a self-deprecating sigh as she swung down from the saddle to join Karla by the fence. "Dropping me out here did the trick."

"Does that mean you're ready to come back to work?"

Karla had weighed the asking of the question carefully. Sara weighed her reply with just as much care. She shook her head. "Not yet. I'm not sure if I ever will be."

Tears filled Karla's eyes, prompting a welling of moisture in her own. "Hey, none of that. I'll work it out, Karla. I just need a little more time. Come on," she coaxed, forcing a smile. "Before we both get all watery, why don't you go on up to the house and say hello to Lana and Cody while I put this little girl away? Then we can have a heart to heart."

"I'd heard about nurses breaking," Sara confessed later, after she and Karla had gotten comfortable in the living room of her little casa. She'd showered and changed, and now that the ice was broken, she'd relaxed. This was her best friend. She could tell Karla everything, and always had. "I just never thought it would happen to me."

"It can happen to any of us."

"Not to you," Sara said matter-of-factly.

"But that's not to say it wouldn't have if I hadn't had Lance. I sometimes wonder if that isn't part of your problem. You don't have anyone to share the load."

That much Sara had begun to recognize as truth. Her daddy hadn't wanted her going into nursing in the first place. Her mother, long divorced from her father and living in Houston, had been appalled. Because of their attitudes, she'd been determined to be the best. That determination might have been her downfall.

"Well, just so you know I'm not acting on any nasty impulses anymore," Sara said with a sheepish grin. "I've got a handle on one problem. Booze was never my style, anyway. I don't even like it. I can't imagine why I thought I'd find any answers there. The hangovers are hell, and the highs don't balance out the lows."

Karla's smile relayed her relief and approval.

"Now," Sara added with a warped grin, "if I could just figure out what I want to do now that I'm all grown up."

She left the thought dangling, as much out of frustration as out of disgust.

"You'll figure it out," Karla assured her. "I guess the immediate question is, where? I know you aren't ready to come back to work, but are you ready to come back to Dallas?"

Sara took a slow sip of her iced tea and leaned her head back against the sofa. "If you'd asked me that last week, I'd have had my bags packed and been planted in the back seat of your car before you could say 'Don't you want to think about this?' Now, I'm content to stay put. At least for a little while longer."

"And how's Tucker going to feel about that, do you think?"

One corner of her mouth tipped up. "Not too hot, I'd say."

"You two didn't hit it off too well, I take it."

That assumption brought an actual laugh. "Were we supposed to? If I recall, my mission was to sit on my duff and collect myself and stay the heck away from Mr. Love-'em-and-leave-'em Lambert.''

"But you didn't?"

She snorted. "Not quite."

Karla studied her with a frown. "I don't think I like that look."

Sara stared at her iced tea, avoiding Karla's eyes. "Tell me about Tucker," she said after a hesitant silence.

Karla's frown deepened. "I *know* I don't like *that* look. And I like the question even less. The less you know about him, the better," she said, after gauging Sara's expression more critically. "Look, he may be my friend, and I trust him, or I wouldn't have left you with him, but I'm telling you, Sara, he's not the kind of man you want to get involved with."

"Who said I wanted to get involved?"

"That look in your eyes says so. Oh, Lord," she muttered, rising from the sofa and dragging her hand through her hair. "I don't believe this. I told Lance leaving you here with him wasn't a good idea."

"He's not such a bad guy, Karla," Sara said, meeting her eyes evenly. "And I'm a big girl. I can handle it."

"Sara," Karla pleaded, sitting down beside her again and taking her hand, "you came here to heal. A fast, hot affair with Tucker is not going to help you accomplish that—and trust me, an affair is all the commitment you'll ever get out of him. When it's over, he'll only have compounded the hurt, and you'll be further from pulling yourself together."

Sara looked away, suspecting her friend was right, yet unable to leave it alone. "Tell me about him, Karla," she insisted softly. "Tell me everything you know."

Five

The Griffins stayed for supper. Everyone laughed and relaxed and enjoyed each other's company. Everyone except Tucker and Karla.

For all Sara's insistence that she wasn't interested in Tucker, Karla still felt uneasy. And for all the grousing Tucker was doing over getting rid of Sara, the looks she saw him cast her way when he thought no one was watching had Karla drawing the wildest conclusions imaginable.

"What do you think?" Karla asked Lance as they pulled away late that evening, reluctantly leaving Sara behind.

"About what?"

"Don't play dumb with me. You know what."

Lance grinned. "Well," he said slowly, "I think

Tucker was a little too insistent that we take Sara with us when we left—and a little too miffed when we didn't.''

"Which means?''

"Which means that since I've never seen our free-wheeling friend this upset over a woman, the chances are good he's in deep dirt over this one.''

Karla chewed on her lower lip. "That's what I was afraid of. Sara's in deep, too, though she won't admit it.''

Lance laughed. "It's out of our hands, babe. So there's no use worrying over what might or might not happen. Besides, I'm not so sure it's such a bad idea. After all, if we'd listened to our friends and family, we'd never have ended up together.''

"That's different.''

"How was it different?''

"You needed me," she said, sounding smug.

He conceded the point with a soft look. "And what makes you think they don't need each other?''

She considered his question in frowning silence as the vast Texas landscape swept past the car windows, blending to a purple-and-pearl dusk.

They knocked off work on Sunday. It was one of the rare weekends without a competition. They all needed the rest. Lana and Tag needed time together. With each other and with Cody. Tucker insisted.

He had a need or two of his own—specifically, he needed time away from them and the reminder that what those two kids had together would forever be out of reach for him. Mostly, though, he needed time away from Sara Stewart.

Damn the woman. She made him hot and horny. Angry and disgusted. More than that, she made him think. And feel. He didn't want to do either, not because of a woman. All he wanted to experience with a woman was sex, he told himself, working hard on believing it. It was all he was good at giving—just like his old man.

A muscle in his jaw worked as he left the house early and walked to the horse barn to saddle up Poco. At least he recognized his weakness and dealt with it. Unlike the old man, he wouldn't make promises he couldn't keep. That way, no one got hurt. Sara made him think about promises. She made him think and wonder if maybe he hadn't settled for a little less than he could get. If maybe he wasn't worthy of a little more than he'd always figured he deserved.

He was about to swing into the saddle and get as far away from her and her expectations as he could when he sensed he had company. His shoulders stiffened as the light morning breeze wafted in through the open barn door, bringing her scent with it.

Timing was everything in this old world, he thought with a resigned sigh, and forced himself to face her. Standing in the open doorway, backlit by daylight and shadow, she looked small and fragile and as refreshing as the day which was sunshine-bright and unseasonably cool. And as sexy as ever-loving sin, with her soft, dark curls tugged and lifted by the summer breeze and her cinnamon-and-spice eyes shaded by a small, uncertain smile.

He was certifiably loco for not having personally shoved her into the back seat of Lance's car last night. He'd told Lance he wanted her gone. He'd told him to get her the hell off Blue Sky. For all the good it had done him.

"Working today?" she asked, in a tone as tentative as her stance and as soft as her skin.

"Ridin' fence," he said, tearing his gaze away and turning back to the stud.

"Sounds like fun."

He heard the hint of wistfulness in her voice. Heard it, and refused to succumb to it. "Last I knew, checking fence was not fun," he said gruffly. "It's a dull, boring job."

"A little company might make it fun," she countered, and offered him the suggestion of another smile when he scowled at her over his shoulder. "At the very least, it might make it a little less boring."

He wasn't up to answering that smile. He wasn't up to issuing an invitation. He wasn't up to any of this. Not the things she made him feel. Not the things she made him want and he sure as hell couldn't have.

"Hey, Lambert," she said, moving up beside him. "Lighten up, would you? And for God's sake, would you quit scowling? That's all you've done for the past four days."

He turned and glared at her. The woman didn't have the sense to cut and run. She just shook her head and grinned. When he gave her his best you're-pushing-the-hell-out-of-this snarl, he was damned if she didn't laugh.

"Look," she said, working hard at pulling a straight face, "you've made your position clear, okay? You don't want me here. You thought that by now I'd be gone. Well, I'd be sorry about that, if I really thought I was putting you out. But the fact of the matter is, you could use my help right now. And frankly..."

She trailed off, then looked away, as if she were struggling with her next words. When she spoke again, all traces of her smile were gone. "Frankly, I could use a little more time to...to get myself back together." Her voice had gone achingly soft, and her eyes a little misty with emotion. "I figure, maybe it makes for an even trade."

Yeah, he thought in grim silence. It makes us even. But it didn't make it easy. He did not want to hurt this woman. If she stayed much longer, he couldn't guarantee that he wouldn't.

He faced her with reluctance and, for the first time, with complete honesty. "There's more to it than that, Sara, and you know it."

She shifted uncomfortably, tucked her hands in her hip pockets and let out a deep breath. "Yeah. There's more to it than that."

For the longest time, he stood there. Steeped in wants, bound by regrets, determined to give in to neither.

"I'm attracted to you. Physically," he added, with an emphasis meant to discourage the notion of any further possibilities. "But that's where it ends," he added for good measure. "I'm not interested in any other kind of a relationship."

He told himself he was being truthful, promised himself he meant it, and that the hurt that flashed across her face in the moment before she hid it didn't affect him.

"Following through on that attraction and acting on it are two different things," he continued, telling himself this was for her benefit, not his.

"It's not going to happen, Sara. It doesn't matter how much I want it or how much you think you want it. It's just not going to happen. Involvement with you would only be another headache, and I've got enough of those already. So believe me when I say I'm not interested."

"You're not interested," she repeated, after a long, humming moment. She shrugged, then met his eyes with an openness that fractured the hell out of his control. "Fine. I can live with that. In fact, I appreciate your honesty. It clears the air. And you're right. A physical relationship is a bad idea. Actually, knowing where you stand on that is kind of a relief."

The return of that mischievous light in her eye had him narrowing his with suspicion. "Relief?"

"Yeah. Don't take this personally, cowboy, but you're really not my type, anyway. Feel better, now?"

He gave her a hard stare. Was she sassing him? Or was she telling it straight? One possibility was as unsettling as the other.

"So, since we're clear on that issue," she went on, before he could decide how to deal with her flashing eyes and sexy-as-silk grin, "is there anything stopping us from sharing a beautiful day?

"Oh, come on, what do you say?" she coaxed, absently stroking the stud's muzzle as Tucker stood there clenching his jaw. "Can you use some company, or do you want me to take a hike?"

What he wanted was for her to leave him alone. What he wanted was to get her out of reach. What he wanted was to take her to his bed and into his heart and tell her things he'd never told another living soul. Which proved his earlier conclusion. He was just plain out of his head. Which, he accepted fatalistically, explained the next words out of his mouth.

"I'll saddle up Jez," he said, after a long-suffering sigh. "Go get your boots and hat."

To Sara's surprise, they rode in a pleasant, companionable silence for the better part of an hour. During that hour, an awareness of her affinity for the ranch, like her slow, heart-stalling acceptance of her growing feelings for Tucker, crept up on her.

She hadn't realized how deeply the wide-open spaces had settled into her blood in the short time she'd been at Blue Sky. It had just happened, the way a cool sunset was the inevitable end of a yellow-hot day. The way the comfort of a deep sleep was the reward for hours of restless denial.

Like the man at her side, whose brooding good looks and haunting blue eyes spoke of secrets and sadness and drew him into her heart, even as her head cautioned her to keep her distance.

She'd lied through her teeth to get him to take her with him. Just as he'd lied about his feelings for her. She hadn't believed him. She felt his longing with her heart, saw his yearnings with her eyes. She accepted what was happening here, and was determined to make him accept it, too.

It wasn't going to be easy. Tucker Lambert was like the country they surveyed, both wild and beautiful, both beckoning and a little bit dangerous. From the gently rolling hills to the cracked creek basins, sage to saw grass, she was enthralled. Just as she was enthralled with this good-time Charlie with the heartbreak-blue eyes and the Texas-size charm.

She knew it wasn't wise. She even knew she'd probably end up hurt. He'd become a total enigma to her, much harder to deal with than when she'd thought he was little more than a flirt in tight denim. There was more to the man. So much more than he wanted anyone to see. She was determined to find out what he was hiding…what part of him needed protecting so diligently that he guarded it at his own expense.

That was why she'd lied. The only way to get to know the real Tucker Lambert, she'd realized, was to convince him that her feelings were as shallow as the creek bed they'd just crossed. Trouble was, she already suspected they ran much deeper. Black-water deep. Deep-water dangerous. And she was in way over her head.

Go figure, she thought with a sigh of total defeat as she admired his unrivaled good looks and his smooth grace in the saddle. She'd never been one to fall for a pretty face. She'd never gone for the flash and fire.

But seeing him today, looking for all the world like an outlaw who'd just posed for a calendar or a wanted poster, she found herself slipping deeper under his spell. The memory of each haunted, hollow look when he'd tried to physically and mentally set her away from him only made her want to heal a hurt that she suspected cut as deep and as painful as her own.

He turned and caught her staring. She smiled. Then smiled even wider when he looked away, a black scowl back in place that made his ruggedly handsome face even more appealing.

"I've been wondering," she began, starting on ground she felt was fairly level, "is Tucker your given name?"

He hesitated for a moment, as if giving over that small piece of himself might be an irreversible step in the wrong direction. In the end, he gave up the information with a throwaway shrug that suggested it wasn't really important.

"I'm told that when I was a kid I was a bit of a hellion."

"Imagine that," she said, softening her sarcasm with a smile.

He gave her a hard glare that warned her that if

she wanted to hear this she'd best keep her smart mouth under control.

It shouldn't have, but his irritation tickled her. Good, she thought. Let him get riled. Maybe he'd let go a little and level with her. Maybe he'd lose that control he'd latched on to like a lifeline.

With a supplicating look that she had to bury her tongue in her cheek to maintain, she promised to oblige him.

"Anyway," he continued, in her estimation trying to sound grumpy but fighting a glimmer of amusement at her cheeky attitude, "my mother was fond of telling everybody within earshot that I plumb tuckered her out." He shrugged again. "Guess it stuck."

It suited him somehow, and at the same time fueled her desire to fill in the blank spaces that Karla, digging in her heels, had refused to flesh out.

"And am I going to have to guess your given name?" she asked, wondering if she was going to have to pry every piece of information out of him with a crowbar.

"John," he said flatly.

Her smile faded as a shadow crossed his face. A cold, dark chill shuddered through her when he added in a hard, emotionless voice, "After my old man."

This, she could see, was forbidden ground. At least for now. Old hurts, far from numb, were etched on his face, icing his eyes over at the mention of his father.

"And Tag?" she asked, before the silence could become unbreachable, "Is there a story there, too?"

His shoulders relaxed a little. "That had more to do with me. The day he took his first step, he started following me around like stink on a skunk. Tagging along everywhere. Never letting me out of his sight. Guess it stuck, too.

"Tom," he added, anticipating her next question. "After my mother's father. Any other part of my case history you're of a need to know, Miz Stewart?" he asked, his voice full of sarcasm, but gentled a bit by a reluctant softness in his eyes.

"Only why you resort to calling me Miz Stewart when you get your back up."

He just grunted. Fixing his gaze on the fence in the distance, he tugged his Resistol farther down on his brow, kneed the stallion and rode away at an easy lope.

Sara sat for a moment, watching him go. Jezibel fought the bit, wanting to go after them. *So you think you can run away from me, do you, cowboy?*

"Not in this lifetime," she murmured under her breath. Tucking her own hat a little tighter, she gave the mare loose rein.

They caught up with Tucker as he topped a gentle knoll and reined to a stop. Together, in a silence that was edgy yet oddly comfortable, they looked back over the land they'd traveled to the cluster of buildings nestled in the midst of the plains. The nucleus of Blue Sky.

The stucco-and-brick ranch house, with its wide veranda and red tile roof, sparkled like a jewel in the midmorning sun. The little casa Tag and Lana shared, and the matching dwelling where she spent her nights, were miniature replicas of the ranch house, flanking it at right angles on either side. She tugged off her hat, shaking her dark chestnut hair free and brushing it back from her face with her fingers.

Closer to the sprawling barn and the inside and outside riding arenas, the currently unoccupied bunkhouse added the final touches to an operation that was both well thought-out and constructed with no lack of expense.

"It's beautiful," she said, her appreciation reflected in her voice, as well as her words.

"Wait till you see it in the spring," he said, apparently without realizing that the statement implied she'd be around that long. "It's so green then. The magnolias and bluebonnets and sage fill the air with scent and color."

"It sounds pretty," she said, thinking that even the dried earth and yellowed grass speckled with the thatches of bobbing black-eyed Susans and the fencerows dotted with occasional clusters of sunflowers were as pretty as pretty could get.

"Sometimes," he said, so low that she wondered if he realized he'd spoken out loud, "sometimes, I still have trouble believing it's mine."

"Because you didn't think you'd ever find the right setup?"

One side of his mouth tipped up in a lazy, laconic smile. "Because I never figured an operation this pricey was within my reach. Poor boys who grew up mucking stalls and cooling down horses don't usually find their way past the bunkhouse,'' he added, anticipating her next question.

"Poor boys?'' she repeated, hoping to keep the lines of communication open.

He crossed his hands over the pommel and regarded her with a considering once-over. "Poor boys whose mommas do other people's wash to pay the rent and keep food on the table. Poor boys who grow up living from hand to mouth and drift from one dead-end job to another.''

She heard the bitterness that lay just below the surface of his matter-of-fact delivery and knew that now wasn't the time to probe. "You're not drifting anymore.''

"No. I'm not,'' he agreed, stern-faced as he looked back across the sprawling ranch land. "But I would be, if it wasn't for Lance.''

"Lance?''

He turned back to her, clearly considering how much he was going to reveal. "Lance is the money behind Blue Sky. He's not only my friend, he's my bankroll.''

This was news. She'd known Tucker and Lance were friends, but she hadn't know they were business associates.''

"So you were right when you figured out he had me up against the wall when he and Karla brought you here. I couldn't turn you away. No way could I tell him no to anything. Even to dumping a small woman with a big problem on my doorstep.''

There was no judgment in his words, just a blunt

statement of fact. A fact she was working hard on overcoming. But not right now. Right now, she was working on him.

"I can't imagine Lance applying that kind of pressure."

He smiled grimly. "He didn't. At least not the kind of pressure you think. He'd never do that. He'd never use his financial clout to try to influence me. He's too much of a straight shooter for that."

"Then why did you agree to let me stay?"

"Because he's my friend. And so is Karla. With that kind of friendship, you don't pull punches—or turn down any requests."

She nodded. "I know what you mean. It's like that for me, too. Karla and I go back to college. She was the poor girl from the wrong side of the tracks and I was the rich bitch who was bucking tradition. Talk about opposite ends of the social spectrum. Yet somehow, we formed a bond that will never break."

"Well, there you go," he said, nudging the stud into a walk. "You and Karla. Me and Lance. Stranger than truth."

She clucked to Jezibel and matched his lazy pace beside him. "How did you and Lance meet?"

"Don't you ever get tired of asking questions?"

He wanted to sound irritated, but he just couldn't pull it off. That knowledge spurred her on.

"Let's just say I find you fascinating, Mr. Lambert," she said with a cheeky grin.

He snorted. "Let's just say I find you nosy."

"That, too," she agreed, playing for a smile and finally getting one.

He let out a deep breath, gave up and gave in. "How did we meet? It's a long story."

"Just your luck, I've got plenty of time."

"Just my luck," he grumbled with a halfhearted scowl, and then, for reasons she didn't want to dissect and praised the gods for divining, he started talking without guarding every word he said.

The story he told her was incredible. It was a story she'd known part of but had never dreamed Tucker had been a party to. Now it all made sense. Karla had come to work one morning nearly bubbling over with excitement over this incredible hunk her friend had dragged into ER the day before, when Sara was off duty. That hunk was Lance Griffin, and he'd been mugged on a city street. Karla's friend, who had found Lance beaten unconscious, was Tucker.

"I wonder why Karla didn't tell me," she said, almost to herself.

"Tell you what?"

"That it was you who'd brought Lance into the ER that night."

"Probably figures it didn't matter. It was an accident that I was the one who found him. Just a twist of fate."

"That ended up with Lance and Karla falling in love," she pointed out. "Not to mention you probably saved his life."

He rolled a shoulder, uncomfortable with the

weight of that conclusion. "If not me, someone else would have taken care of him."

"Maybe," she said, considering. "And maybe he would have died out there if you hadn't played the Good Samaritan."

"Hey—don't go pinning any medals on my chest. It's no big deal, okay?"

"Lance must have thought it was a big deal."

"Yeah, well, Lance is in love. A man gets a little addlebrained when he's in that state."

She laughed out loud. "He looked pretty sound of mind to me yesterday. And now I understand the basis for your friendship."

"And the reason I've got more than a wish and a prayer and an illusive piece of *blue sky* to hold on to. I've got the real thing. Lance figured he owed me, and when the ranch came up for sale three years ago, he looked me up and made me an offer only a fool would refuse."

"And Tucker Lambert's no fool, right?"

Wrong, Tucker thought as he searched those summer-warm eyes of hers and realized he'd told her more about himself than he'd ever intended to tell. It struck him like a kick from a mad calf that he'd enjoyed the telling.

"If that were true," he said, fully intending to back away from that unnerving scrap of reality and close himself off again, "I'd have done something with my life long before Lance came on the scene."

"Possibly." She eyed him again, with that thoughtful expression that told him she didn't buy what he'd just said. "And possibly an opportunity just hadn't presented itself."

"Darlin'," he said, determined to set her straight, "this Texan doesn't let any opportunity go by. Just ask anyone who knows me."

"And who might that be?" Her eyes were clear and probing. "Who do you let get close enough to know you, Tucker? I'm not talking about the bad-boy brawler who swaggers like he doesn't give a damn and claims he tumbles anything in skirts. I'm talking about the man who gets involved. The man who saves strangers at risk to his own safety. The man who puts up with wayward nurses who've lost their sense of direction.

"I'm talking about the man who not only drops what he's doing to pull his kid brother out of trouble, but takes him and his wife and baby under his wing to make sure they have a chance together."

He felt momentarily stunned before he muttered, "Someone's got a big mouth."

"And someone else has a tendency to sell himself short."

He worked his jaw and looked away. What he'd done—for Lance, and for Tag and Lana—was a direct result of fate and circumstances. What he'd done for Sara was the payback for a debt. It had nothing to do with character, or with duty or responsibility. Why couldn't she get that through her head?

"How did you meet Karla?" she asked, before he had a chance to set her straight.

"How did you get so pushy?"

"Practice." She grinned at him. "And persistence."

He shook his head, determined not to give in to an exasperated grin. "And to think I was glad when you finally decided to talk."

"Well, like you said, there's a downside to everything."

Their eyes met and held for a moment so long it seemed to stretch into next week, as he thought about what had prompted him to utter those words. It had been after she promised him he didn't have to worry about getting "accosted" by moonlight again. Only *accosted* wasn't the word that came to mind. *Seduction* was. A slow, sensual seduction that had stirred his blood and seared to his groin and kept him awake and aching for her every night since.

"I met Karla the same way she met Lance," he said, steering away from the awareness in her eyes and the trouble courting it could bring him. "Karla patched me up when a buddy dragged me into ER one night when we closed down a bar. I was known to get in a brawl or two back then."

"And to break a few hearts?" she added with quiet speculation.

"My stock-in-trade, darlin'," he said, taking the opportunity to drive his point home. "Always has been. Always will be."

"If you say so."

Her look was doubtful and her tone unconvinced as her gaze drifted away. She nodded toward a lone live oak a quarter mile ahead. "So, are you still up to living a little dangerously?"

Though he was glad for the change of subject, he couldn't say he much cared for the look in her eyes. "What do you have in mind?"

"Beating the pants off you," she told him with a sassy laugh as she cued Jezibel with her knees, hung on to her hat and tore off across the knoll at breakneck speed.

Poco reacted to the challenge, dancing and rearing and champing at the bit to run. Cursing her recklessness, Tucker gave Poco his head, leaned forward in the saddle and let the stallion flat-out fly.

The big sorrel was bred for speed and athleticism, the mare for endurance. She didn't stand a chance. He caught up to her with a sixteenth of a mile to go. Both horses and riders were winded from the exertion and the excitement when they pulled up under the tree.

"That big boy can run," she said, laughing, as she slid off Jezibel's back and ground-reined the mare.

Tucker swung out of the saddle. He rounded on her, shoved back his hat with an agitated punch of his thumb and propped his fists on his hips. "And you don't have the sense—"

"God gave a rock. I know," she said, cutting him off with a teasing laugh as her eyes sparkled in the July sun.

"That was a stupid thing to do, *cowboy!*"

"Yeah, but you've got to admit, it was a hell of a ride."

Yeah, he thought, cooling himself down, he had to admit that it was. Being with her was a ride. A bona fide out-of-control jumble onto wild, uncharted ground.

He'd never felt out of control around a woman before. Never felt this close to the edge of letting go. Of his thoughts, of his feelings, of an insistent, building urge to let her lead the way, and damn the consequences.

"So..." She dropped to the soft grass, leaning back on an elbow while she caught her breath. "Have you always trained cutters?" Tugging off her hat, she shook her dark chestnut hair free and brushed it back from her face with a sweep of her fingers.

He squinted against the sun, knowing it wasn't wise to join her, accepting that he'd never been a wise man. Ground-reining Poco near the mare, he pulled a thermos from a saddlebag and joined her in the shade.

"Always?" He unscrewed the cap and offered her a drink. She shook her head. "No. I haven't always trained them. Have I always wanted to? Yeah. But before I found Blue Sky, I did anything I could to earn a buck."

He took a long, deep swallow of the ice-cold water, then wiped his mouth with the back of his hand, trying not to watch as she rolled over on her stomach and laid her cheek on her crossed wrists, facing him.

"Such as?" she prompted.

He snorted, leaned back on his elbows and crossed his ankles. He studied his boots with a frown. "Nothing worth talking about."

"I doubt that," she insisted, the interest in her tone making him look at her. "Tell me."

She looked so uncomplicated lying there. So soft and vulnerable, mellow and trusting. And interested. In something other than his body and his looks. Another first. Another puzzle—why it affected him so.

Tucker wished he felt so uncomplicated. He couldn't stop looking at her. When her eyelids drifted shut, he gave up trying.

Her lashes were thick and dark, a lacy web of silk that kissed the ridge of her cheeks as she relaxed in the dappled sunlight beneath the Texas sun and the shady tree.

She prompted him again, sleepily. "Tell me, Tucker."

"I've done everything from road construction to working offshore oil rigs, to laying brick, to busting broncs," he said finally.

She fought it, but couldn't stop a huge yawn. "Yet you ended up here."

"Yet I ended up here." He echoed her sleepy words softly and wondered, as he watched the tension ease out of her limbs and a lazy fatigue take over, exactly where "here" was.

He swallowed hard and looked out over the land he'd someday call his own. Yeah. He was here. Doing what he'd always wanted to do. Living like he'd always wanted to live.

And wondering why the fact that he couldn't keep her with him made him feel so damn alone.

Six

The thick grass did little to cushion the hard-packed earth beneath her. Yet the breeze felt so sweet, and her thoughts were drifting so unstructured and free that Sara hung on tight to the lethargic tug of sleep.

Tucking her arms beneath her chest, she turned her face away from the feathery flutter tickling her cheek.

"Fire."

The word filtered through a muzzy haze. She ignored it, then swatted at her neck, where that persistent little tickle insisted on pestering her.

"Stampede."

She was considering getting cranky when she recognized the Texas-slow voice as Tucker's. Reluctantly she opened one eye. And abruptly closed it against a blinding spear of sunlight peeking through the breeze-stirred leaves of the oak.

"Chocolate."

She groaned and grudgingly gave it up. "All right, all ready. I'm awake."

"Interesting," he said, in a measuring, amused tone, "that it was the mention of food, not fear for your life, that finally did the trick."

She rolled onto her side, blinked the sleep out of her eyes and glanced pointedly at the piece of grass dangling between his fingers.

"Interesting," she countered, sitting up slowly and stretching the kinks and stiffness out of her limbs, "that a grown man would resort to schoolboy tricks."

Leaning back on his hand, he hitched up a knee and draped his arm over it. "Seemed kinder that way," he said, tossing the grass aside.

She narrowed her eyes, suspicious of the ornery glint in his. "Kinder than what?"

"Oh, say…" He angled a look toward the thermos. "Kinder than dumping cold water down your back."

She might not be fully awake, and she might be reading more into it than was wise, but she recognized flirting when she saw it. And Mr. Lambert, though he might claim he didn't want to, was definitely flirting with her.

She considered the pleasant implication of that notion, considered the thermos, then him. "Umm. I'm humbled by your thoughtfulness. And I could use some of that now."

He handed it over. Their fingers touched, a little

longer than was necessary, and, she could see by the look on his face, a little longer than he thought was wise.

"You have creases on your cheek," he said finally, when their gazes had touched and tangled for even longer than that telling contact of their fingers.

"And a crick in my neck," she added, warmed by his soft, indulgent smile. Hiding her pleasure behind a yawn, she gave a full-body shudder, then drank. "How long have I been out?"

"Not long." His words were dismissive, but his tone told her it had been long enough for him to do some thinking. And some watching. And maybe have a change of heart.

"Sorry." She grimaced as she hunched her shoulders, then rolled her head on her neck. "I guess I wasn't very good company."

"Oh, I don't know." One corner of his mouth tipped up in a lazy grin. "I kind of appreciated the silence."

"Yeah?" she asked archly. "Well appreciate this." She dipped her fingers into the thermos cup and flicked water in his face.

Her surprise attack choked a laugh out of him. "So, she gets cranky when she doesn't get her full nap in."

She smiled, catlike and coy and without an ounce of repentance. "She gets even."

Refilling the thermos cup, she eyed him with a calculated once-over that relayed every devilish, dangerous thought in her head. "Care for a little *more* cold water, cowboy?"

"I wouldn't do that." Though he smiled sweetly, his eyes backed up his warning with a promise that the consequences of any rash action would not go easy on her.

"Maybe *you* wouldn't." She gave him a long, considering look. "But I'm not you."

Then she flung the water at him, hitting his chest dead-center.

Eyes wide, she held her breath and waited to see if he'd make good on his threat.

He didn't say a word. Just looked down at his wet shirt, then up at her. His smile, when it came, was as unexpected as his speed. Both caught her off guard when he lurched for her.

With a surprised scream, she rolled out of his reach, shot to her feet and ran like hell.

He caught her just as she reached Jezibel.

She shrieked again and, laughing, tried to skitter away from him. He was too fast. And too strong. And too determined to make her pay.

Banding one strong arm around her waist, he slung her across his hip like a sack of feed and carried her, kicking and pleading, back to their spot under the tree.

"You are in *sooo* much trouble," he promised as he plopped her down on her rump and loomed over her. Straddling her hips, he dropped to his knees and pushed her to her back. With his strong thighs riding either side of her ribs, he banded her wrists above her head.

"I'm sorry I'm sorry I'm sorry!" she cried in a

wheedling tone as she bucked and twisted beneath his weight.

"Are you, now?" He looked thoroughly unconvinced and maddeningly arrogant as he smiled his captor's smile above her.

"Yes...*yes!*" she insisted with a desperate, wary cry as he bound her wrists with one hand and reached for the thermos with the other.

"Just how sorry would that be, Miz Smartmouth?" His grin was as smug as sin, and his blue eyes were dancing as he tipped the open thermos at a threatening angle over her head.

"Sorrier than Dan Quayle when he went head-to-head with Murphy Brown," she said on a laugh, then shrieked again when he let a trickle of liquid ice spill onto her throat. "You're going to pay for this, Lambert."

"This from a woman who is in no position to be making threats." He chuckled when she glared at him. "Now, come on, darlin', you can do better. How sorry are you?"

"Sorrier than your sorry hide," she sputtered, and bucked again, then gasped when her own wild gyrations jarred his arm and sent water spilling all over her chest.

Eyes wide against the shock and cold, she went very still. Above her, he did the same as his gaze surveyed what their horseplay and the water had done.

She didn't have to look down to see that her pale blue knit shirt clung to her breasts, emphasizing their fullness. She didn't have to see the damage to know her nipples were defined by wet cotton, hard and peaked with cold and a quivering awareness of Tucker's heated gaze.

All she had to do was look in his eyes and watch cool blue change to a slow-burning flame. All she had to do was feel the heat of him pressing against her hips and his grip on her wrists change from imprisonment to caress.

Tucker felt like he'd been blindsided...by a fire burning out of control, by a herd of stampeding horses.

He'd pulled some stupid stunts in his life. He'd made some critical errors. But flirting with Sara Stewart this sunny afternoon had been just plain dumb. It had led him straight to disaster.

He'd known it when he started. Yet he hadn't been able to stop it. And as he gazed down on her fever-bright eyes, watched the gentle rise and fall of her breasts, the wet cotton covering them more enticing than bare skin, he knew it was too late to undo the damage. Too late to turn back. Too late to stop what he'd never intended to start.

"Some people just can't seem to stay out of cold water," he said in a gritty voice, his gaze skating hotly from her breasts to her eyes, then back to her breasts again.

As one, their thoughts drifted back to the night when he'd held her, wet and naked and shivering, the cold water drenching them as heavy as their regrets.

Regrets. He'd had his share of them about

her…and it looked like he was going to have some more.

"I'm sorry," he murmured into a thick silence that was charged with awareness and desire and had nothing to do with wet clothes.

"That…that's supposed to be my line." She forced a shaky smile, then, watching his eyes, drew her lower lip between her teeth.

If the picture she made lying there, her chestnut hair spread thick and wild around her head, wet cotton clinging to her breasts, hadn't been enough to send him over the edge, the sight of those even white teeth biting into the plump flesh of her lip alone would have completely unhinged him.

"I warned you to keep your distance." It came out on a growl as his breath became labored and his chest expanded. "I told you what would happen if you didn't."

His voice relayed his deepest wants, betrayed his resolve to resist her. His desire was too strong to be swayed. As he loomed above her, he saw in her eyes that she knew. The horseplay was over. Another kind of play had begun.

"Lucky for me…" She paused, searching his face as his internal flame inched closer to flash point. "Lucky for me you don't have any intention of following through with this…this physical attraction you have for me."

Slowly, slowly, with the summer breeze tickling the back of his neck and her brown eyes burning into his soul, he lowered his mouth to her breast.

"And lucky for me," he murmured, catching the bead of her nipple between his teeth and teasing it through wet cotton and lace, "I'm not your type."

She groaned and arched and offered. And it pushed him over the edge. He plundered her breast with his mouth, playing his tongue across her nipple, finessing it to a sweet, budding hardness.

She pulled against the hand shackling her wrists and pleaded with him. "I want to touch you."

"Oh, no, darlin'." With hedonistic languor, he inched his mouth away and watched her fire flicker, then burst into flame. "You may have started this little game, but I'm going to finish it. And I'm going to make the rules.

"I set the pace, sweet Sara. I say when. I say how. And right now, I say no."

Pinning her hands on the ground above her head, he lowered his mouth over hers. His tongue probing. His teeth scraping. His deep growl of pleasure both threat and hunger and a soulful promise that he'd just begun.

He seduced her mouth with tender kisses and whispered urgings that coaxed her to let him delve inside. With a sweetly savage moan, a softly sensual sigh, she opened for him. He stroked her boldly with his tongue, scattered nipping bites to her jaw and the slender arch of her throat, devouring and possessing, leaving her panting and wanting. Leaving him aching with anticipation, breaking with need.

"Tucker." She sucked in a breath of frustration

and begged again to be freed. "Let me go. I want to touch you."

Again he denied her, brushing his open mouth across her lips as his free hand skated down her ribs to her waist and undid the snap of her jeans.

"Lift up," he ordered as he dragged her shirt out of her jeans and shoved it above her breasts. With a flick of his fingers, he opened the front clasp on her bra.

And then he felt nothing but Sara. Breathed nothing but Sara. Wanted nothing but Sara. His lips against her throat. His hand on her bare breast, kneading, shaping, lifting her to the hunger of his mouth.

She writhed against his heat. Reveled in his aggression as he suckled and sipped and strafed her distended nipple until he felt her pleasure spike to a level that equaled his own.

Finally, he let go of her hands. Finally, he let her touch him…then wondered why he'd waited so long.

Her hands were magic. Her touch was as soft as down, as gentle as spring rain, as she raked her fingers through his hair, stroked his lowered head and held him to her breast in a caress as erotic as it was tender.

With sensual fascination, he experienced the glide of her fingertips as she traced the planes of his jaw and the stubble of his beard, which he feared abraded her tender flesh. The delicious contrast fueled his fire and elicited a moaning gasp from her when he pinched her nipple between his teeth and tugged.

She cried out when he drew her deeply into his mouth. A torrent of hard, electric wanting swept from that point of devouring contact to sluice through his chest and arc to the spot that had grown hard and pulsing for her. But, more than wanting, greater than physical release, emotions eclipsed desire as he held her, plunging him headlong into need.

He'd never let himself pass that threshold with a woman. He'd never let it get that far. He'd settled for sex and called himself blessed. He'd settled for less and called himself lucky. But with Sara, the one thing he'd denied himself his entire life had become the only thing that mattered. To be more than a lover. To share more than a heated tumble. To look forward to more than one night in her bed with no promise of tomorrow.

With a groan, he rolled onto his back, taking her with him. Holding her close, he settled her over his erection with a series of long, lush shifts and the slow, sensual guidance of his hands on her hips. She pressed against him, her eyes telling him how much she ached, how much she wanted, how much she trusted him to do whatever he would do.

His gaze never left her face as he moved his hands to her zipper. His breath stalled thick and heavy in his chest as she dragged her hair out of her eyes and bit her lip between her teeth when he slowly tugged it down.

Her eyes drifted shut on a moan that he answered with one of his own as his hands rose again to her breasts, finding his way through tangled wet cotton and trailing white lace.

"More," he whispered in a ragged rasp.

Without hesitation, she gave. Bracing her hands on either side of his head, she leaned over him, obeying his command, brushing the tips of her breasts across his open mouth. The silk of her hair kissed his face as he nuzzled and licked and took them both to yet a higher plane of need.

And he wondered if he'd ever get enough of her.

With a desperate moan, she reached between their bodies. When she found the snap at his waist, she hesitated, then raised her gaze to his, asking for permission.

He consented with a deep swallow and a slow blink of his eyes as his mind went hazy with wanting her, heavy with emotion, and strained with the weight of keeping both under control.

"Go ahead, darlin'," he murmured, shoving the hair from her eyes and tucking it behind her ear. "I haven't got it in me to say no."

She returned his smile. Confident in her power, bold with desire, she flicked open the brass snap— then froze when a phone rang.

Tucker stopped breathing. He closed his eyes and swore.

Sara's hand stilled, her senses confused, her mind intent on disbelieving. Until she saw his face.

He'd gone as still as silence beneath her.

She stiffened, telling herself, "No way."

But then it rang again, breaking into a silence cluttered with thundering heartbeats and labored breaths.

"What," she asked, knowing she sounded petulant and piqued, "is that?"

"That," he said, letting out a hissing sigh, "is called really rotten timing."

With another muffled oath, he set her away from him, dragged his hands through his hair, then rose to his feet.

"A phone," she said, incredulous, as she watched him stalk toward Poco. Even when he pulled a cellular phone out of a saddlebag, she still didn't want to believe it. "You carry a *phone* in your saddlebag?"

He gave her a dark, twisted grin as he pulled up the antenna. "That's progress."

Sara lowered her head to her upraised knees and fisted both hands in her hair.

"So much for wide-open spaces," she muttered in frustration as he turned his back to her and spoke in hushed, hurried tones. So much for isolation from the real world. So much for making love with Tucker Lambert.

"Come on," he said gruffly as he stuffed the phone back in the saddlebag.

The urgency in his voice set her instantly on edge. She rose quickly to her feet. Fumbling with the clasp of her bra, then stuffing her shirt into her jeans, she zipped up. "What's wrong?"

Leading Poco, he snagged Jezibel's reins and walked toward her. "That was Tag. Lana's got a problem."

Her heart lurched. "With the baby?"

He shook his head. "Don't know. But it sounds like maybe it could be. Tag says she's bleeding and her back is hurting her real bad."

Sara was in the saddle before he got the last word out, kneeing Jezibel into a ground-swallowing run with Tucker fast on her heels.

Sara baled off the mare as they skidded to a stop in front of Tag and Lana's little bungalow. Tag, with a fussing Cody on his hip, met her at the door. His eyes were wild; his hair looked as if it had been raked and reraked by punishing fingers.

"Is she in bed?" she asked. When he nodded, she laid a calming hand on his arm. "That's good. Now what's going on?"

"I don't know. I don't know what to do. She...she's bleeding and...and she's feeling real rough."

"It's okay," she said with a soothing smile, then touched a consoling hand to baby Cody's cheek to settle him.

Just then, Tucker came rushing in the door.

"Take care of them," she said over her shoulder as she headed for the bedroom.

"She's scared," Tag said, stopping her, sounding scared himself.

"I know. We'll take care of her, all right? You just keep yourself together." With a final look toward Tucker, she left them, as silent as stone, behind her.

"Hey there," she said softly when she walked into the bedroom.

Lana turned a tear-stained face on the pillow. Her

huge dark eyes were misty with fear, and her mouth was twisted with the fatigue of worry and pain.

"Not feeling so hot?" Sara asked as she eased a hip onto the bed. She touched a hand to Lana's forehead, then checked her pulse.

Lana shook her head as fresh tears began to trickle down her cheeks. "I...think I'm losing the baby," she said in a raw whisper.

"We can't know that," Sara assured her. Turning down the covers with steady, gentle hands, she tested the tension of Lana's abdominal muscles. Relieved when she felt no undue stress, she smoothed the covers back in place. "Tell me what's happening. Tag says you're bleeding?"

Lana nodded. "When I go to the bathroom. And it burns."

"What else?"

"My back. It...hurts like...like it did when I went into labor with Cody. I'm almost three months along, Sara. I don't want to lose the baby."

"Shush, now." Sara took both of Lana's hands in hers as fresh tears welled up in the younger woman's eyes. "We're not going to let you lose the baby. In fact, I don't think the baby has anything to do with your problem. Honey...have you ever had a urinary tract infection?"

Lana sniffled, then frowned. "I don't think so."

"Well, you need to see a doctor to make sure, but what you're telling me sounds more like a UT than early labor."

"But it hurts so much." Even through the pain and worry, a glimmer of hope flickered in Lana's eyes.

"You're darned right it hurts. And if it is a UT, a little sulphur will take care of it in no time at all. Some cranberry juice might help in the meantime. Do you have any?"

"Yes. I buy it for Cody."

"Well, Cody's mom is going to get a little of it right now." Smiling, she rose from the bed. "I'll get the juice, and then we'll call your doctor and tell him what's going on. Okay?"

Lana nodded shakily. "Do you...do you really think the baby's okay?"

"Is there anything else you're not telling me?"

She shook her head.

Sara smiled. "Then, yeah, I think the baby's okay. And you will be, too. Real soon. Now you sit tight, and I'll be right back."

Three Lambert men met her at the bedroom door, one with sad, soulful eyes and his thumb in his mouth and two with scowls as black as thunderclouds.

"Well?" the brothers asked in unison.

"Well," she said with a thoughtful calm as she ushered them away from the door. "I think she's got herself a raging urinary tract infection."

"What does that mean?" Tag asked anxiously.

"It means she's hurting like the devil but we can take care of it."

"And the baby?"

"The baby's okay."

Tag let out a deep draft of pent-up breath and threw a look of relief over Cody's head to his brother.

"So what do we do?" Tucker asked, ready to help with whatever was necessary.

Sara was all too glad to swing into action. Tag got the juice while Sara and Lana talked to Lana's obstetrician, who concurred with Sara's assessment. With instructions to Sara to monitor Lana closely in case it was a problem with her pregnancy, he phoned a prescription to the closest pharmacy and set up an appointment for Lana to come to the office tomorrow morning to follow up.

Tucker climbed into the truck and raced at speeds Sara didn't even want to think about to pick up the prescription and bring it back.

Three hours later, with a quart of cranberry juice down her and her first dose of sulfur already easing the discomfort, Lana was sitting up in bed. Tag had lost that haggard look as he sat in a rocker by the bed, little Cody sound asleep in his arms.

From the doorway, Sara observed the three of them with a warm, contented feeling before she slipped out of the house and down to the barns, where Tucker had gone to take care of the horses.

"Everything all right?" he asked when he spotted her walking toward Poco's stall.

She nodded, tucking her hands in her hip pockets. "Yeah. She's doing fine. So is Tag...finally," she added with a grin.

One corner of his mouth tipped up. "Not much in a crisis, is he?"

"He loves her," she said simply.

He sliced her a long, considering look before turning back to the stall. "Yeah. He does."

"These two okay?" she asked, referring to Jezibel and Poco, even though she was more worried about the look in Tucker's eyes. The one that said he was having second thoughts. Then the one that came on its heels and told her he'd decided this afternoon was a mistake and he'd been a fool for letting things go as far as they had.

"No worse for the wear," he said finally. "The exercise did more good than harm."

"And what about our exercise?" she asked, taking a chance that he wouldn't close off from her completely. Hoping against hope that he'd let what had begun between them play itself out. "We didn't finish our...workout."

He turned to face her then. When he saw her mischievous smile, his killer grin slipped reluctantly into place, along with an exasperated I-don't-know-what-to-do-about-you-but-I'm-helpless-to-resist　surrender that turned her heart to mush and her legs to pudding.

"Has that mouth of yours ever gotten you into trouble?"

Her smile broadened to sexy and smug and as full of hell as his stalking gait as he closed the distance between them.

"Not lately," she said, holding his gaze. "But I'm holding out hope that it will."

He stopped a deep breath away from her, devouring

her with his eyes, touching her with his smile. "Oh, it will, darlin'. Bank on it."

"Promises, promises."

"You want promises?" His blue eyes glittered darkly as he moved that final step to meet her. Bracketing her waist with his broad hands, he backed her up against the wall of a stall. "I'll make you a promise. We're going to finish our *workout* just as soon as I can arrange it."

She draped her arms around his neck, all eager anticipation and anxious lover. "No time like the present, I always say."

He laughed and shook his head. "You're trouble, you know that?"

She only smiled.

"Tonight," he insisted, though she could see he thought her idea had merit. "After supper. In my bed." His expression darkened with passion and promise. "Work for you?"

She let out a frustrated breath. "Patience has never been my strong suit."

His eyes, though soft, lost their laughter. He touched a hand to her cheek. "I think you're wrong. I think patience is one of your very strongest suits. You were terrific with Lana. The poor kid was scared to death."

She shrugged. "Just doing my..." Her voice trailed off as realization hit and she let the thought play itself out. It surprised her when it did. "Just doing my job," she finished, amazed at how well the notion fit.

She *had* been doing her job. With empathy and

compassion. With skill and conviction. And it had felt good. For the first time in a very long while, she'd experienced that exhilarating blend of caring and control that had drawn her to her profession in the first place.

"Is she really going to be okay?" she heard Tucker ask through thoughts that had stalled and settled and felt fairly comfortable where they'd landed.

"Yes," she assured him, pleased by her self-discovery and promising herself that later, when she was alone, she would analyze what it all meant. "She's going to be fine. The trip to the doctor tomorrow is a necessary precaution, and she'll feel better, too, after getting reassurance from him.

"In the meantime," she added, turning all her concentration back on him, "I could use a little reassurance of my own."

She lifted her face to his, her eyes flirty and flashing with the heat of remembered passion. "Tonight is a long ways away."

He sucked in a tortured breath. "And getting longer when you look at me like that."

"And touch you like this?" she suggested, unlacing her hands from around his neck and trailing them in a slow, seductive glide down his chest to the waist of his jeans.

"And touch me like that," he whispered on an indrawn breath, then stopped her wandering hands. "Sara...I've got chores to do."

It came out as half plea, half groan. His desperation

brought a smile to her lips and a gentle tug to her heart.

"Me too," she said, conceding. "Hope you don't mind, but I'm the new chef for tonight."

That closed, cautious look slipped back into place. "You don't have to do that," he said with a scowl. "I can throw something together."

"I want to do it. For Lana," she added, reading his mind. Lord, the man was transparent. Playing at love was one thing. But the thought of her playing at setting up house had brought that trapped look to his eyes again.

"Relax, cowboy. I know the parameters, okay? I want to do this for Lana. She needs to know she's not letting anyone down. I can take her to the doctor tomorrow, too. That way, she won't fuss about Tag missing the workouts. And I'll feel better knowing I'm with her, just in case she runs into any trouble on the way there."

He backed away from her, concern darkening his eyes again. "You think there's a chance of that?"

She shook her head. "No. But *she* does. This way, her mind will rest a little easier."

He considered her for a long moment, his scowl turning so grim she began to feel uneasy. "Seems it's starting to look like we might not be able to manage around here without you."

He might have meant it as a compliment. It came out sounding like a concern. Poor baby, he really was having trouble with this. Much as he appreciated her help, he didn't like the idea that they might be coming to rely on her. Reliance implied necessity. Necessity implied commitment—maybe even permanence.

It was dangerous for both of them to be thinking along those lines. Still, she liked the way the notion fit. She liked even more that he was thinking about it—even if it upset him.

Wise up, Stewart, she warned herself as she left him, detouring to check on Lana before heading for the big house to start supper. Tucker was determined to be what he wanted people to think he was. A man who lived for the moment. A man who never committed to tomorrow. A man who wasn't capable of giving more than surface pleasure to a woman who wanted it to sink in to the root.

And she, like a fool, was close to betting her heart that she was the woman who could prove him wrong.

Seven

A week ago, Tucker had sworn he wasn't going to have anything to do with her. Now he wasn't sure he was going to make it through supper, let alone manage to wait until dark.

She sat at a right angle to him at the supper table. Not close enough to touch, too close to ignore. He couldn't help but watch her. The longer he did, the deeper he sank.

With a beguiling tilt of her head, the soft hint of a secret smile, even the subtle flutter and drift of her thick web of lashes, she covertly enticed and flirted and fired his imagination to a fever pitch.

Lord, the woman did things to his head. Things that he'd never have believed he'd be susceptible to. Things that angered him and amused him and split his thoughts in ten different directions. There was a lot to be said for divide-and-conquer tactics, and the longer he sat here watching her, the more he suspected she knew exactly what a tease she was.

She was working him over but good. Her sweet seduction didn't appear practiced. Instead, it seemed guilelessly natural.

Whatever it was, it was effective…a potent assault on his senses and his powers of control.

Fortunately, Tag was so wrapped up in worrying over Lana, and Lana was so intent in convincing both Cody and Tag that she was all right, that Tucker's dilemma didn't register with them—until a warm, bare foot, hidden under the table, slipped up his leg, wedged itself between his thighs and nestled cozily against his fly.

Her sneak attack caught him completely off guard. His entire body went on sexual alert with a jolt so strong it damn near knocked him out of his chair.

He choked on a mouthful of pasta salad.

All eyes snapped toward him.

"You okay, bro?" Tag asked, poised to jump to his feet and slam a broad palm between Tucker's shoulder blades.

Tucker stalled Tag with an open-palm motion that told him to stay put, then gulped down half a glass of milk.

"You'd best slow down, cowboy. It wouldn't do to have two medical emergencies in one day."

This from the sweetly smiling outlaw with the innocent brown eyes and the busy foot.

"No need to hurry," she added with an indulgent smile. "You can take all night if you want to—there's enough to satisfy even you."

If he could have talked, he'd have sworn at her. If he could have moved, he'd have strangled her. As it was, he could only cut her a warning glare—which she responded to by batting her eyes and pressing her inquisitive little foot more snugly against his fly. He did some responding of his own by growing harder and fuller as the little hellion's curling toes and the double meaning of her seemingly innocent words hummed on the air between them.

"I'm glad to hear that," he countered, finally finding his voice and deciding two could play this game. "Because I find I've worked up one heck of an appetite. And as hungry as I am right now, satisfying it just might take all night."

He had the pleasure of seeing her redden beneath that cheeky little smile as she picked up on his thinly veiled meaning. His pleasure intensified, then turned to triumph when she started drawing her adventurous foot away.

He stopped her retreat with a hand on her ankle and a smile as innocuous as the ones she'd been flashing him. Then he tugged her foot back against him.

"This is really good, Sara," Lana said, oblivious of the game-playing going on under the table.

"Yeah," Tucker added, pressing her foot deeper into his heat, then stroking her bare arch with his thumb until she squirmed. "*Real* good."

"G-glad you like it." She shot him a look that

pleaded with him to cut her some slack. "It…it really wasn't any trouble. I was happy to do it."

He wasn't about to let up on her. His eyes danced to hers, his brow arched, challenging, mocking and superior. "Amazing. An accommodating woman. The world could use a few more, right, Tag?" he asked with a male-to-male grin, taking a page from her book and reading it to her.

He knew he was pushing it when the heat in her cheeks radiated to the tips of her pretty ears. The dangerous glint in her eyes was a warning of worse to come. When the soft pressure of her foot turned abruptly into a hard, twisting grind that seemed to say, *Accommodate this, cowboy!* he opted for the wisdom of letting go.

He carefully lifted her foot from his lap and released it when she jerked it back under her chair.

"So what do you think, babe?" Tag asked Lana as he pushed back from the table. "Time to get you back to bed?"

"I'm not an invalid," Lana protested with a patient smile.

"But you are fighting an infection," Sara reminded her. "At the risk of sounding patronizing, even though you're feeling better, you really do need to rest. I can handle the dishes. Cody, too, if you want me to watch him tonight."

"You've done enough," Tag said. "The little guy's about to fall asleep in his mashed potatoes, anyway. Besides…" He leaned down, reached under the table and, with a knowing grin, handed Sara her discarded sandal, "I think you've got enough to keep you busy tonight."

When her cheeks reddened and her eyes flashed guiltily to his, Tucker simply cocked his head and gave her a look that said, *Hey—you started this. You finish it.*

Her way of finishing it was to snatch the sandal from Tag's hand and ignore it.

"Lana," she said, busying herself cleaning up Cody and lifting him out of the high chair, "don't forget to take your meds tonight. And sleep late in the morning. I can fix breakfast and still get you to your doctor's appointment. No fuss, now, and that's final," she added when Lana began to protest. "Tag, you see to it that she does as she's told."

"You heard her, woman," Tag said, helping Lana to her feet, then taking Cody from Sara. "Like it or not, those feet are going up tonight, and they're staying there."

"You'd think I was a baby," Lana grumbled good-naturedly as Tag ushered her out the door.

"Or that somebody cares about you a whole lot," Sara added in a hushed tone.

Only Tucker heard her. Only Tucker saw the poignant blend of longing and affection touch her face as she watched them go. There was yearning in that look, a wistful sadness that touched him far deeper than it should have.

As she always did, she had him thinking impossible

thoughts, exploring infeasible alternatives, wishing this didn't have to end in disappointment for both of them.

Steeped in longings and blindsided by uncertainty, Sara was slow to become aware of Tucker's silence behind her. In the moment when she turned away from the door and found him watching her, though, she sensed he was struggling with the same edgy expectancy she was.

He stood in the kitchen doorway, his shoulder propped lazily against the doorjamb, his booted feet crossed at the ankles, his arms folded over his chest. He was so beautiful she wanted to cry. So intense, she had to force herself to breathe as he studied her with a look that could have been warning or anticipation or equal measures of both.

His eyes were a cool electric blue. His smile was pleasant by design and, if she didn't miss her guess, as close to the edge of control as she'd dare push him.

"You play dangerous games, little girl."

She agreed. She'd pushed the edges of the envelope with that little bit of folly at the supper table. She still couldn't believe how bold she'd been. But he'd been withdrawing again. That sullen look had resettled in his eyes. So she'd shocked him—and herself—but, by doing so, had kept the situation light.

After all, that was what he claimed he wanted. Playful sex, no heavy commitments.

It was a lie. She could feel it in her bones. He cared about her. He was just too afraid to admit it.

So she'd played. She wasn't sure she had the

strength to confront his will, anyway. After all, it wasn't strength that had landed her here at Blue Sky. It was weakness. Maybe it was weakness that was propelling her now. Maybe she should step back and look at her motives a little more deeply.

Common sense certainly tipped the scales in favor of walking away. But common sense had little to do with need, a need for Tucker that lay heavy and immediate and in the end sent her rushing full bore toward disaster.

"So what's life without a little danger?" she finally managed, meeting his eyes. Her words sounded brave—trouble was, her voice betrayed her. Without the sun and the summer breeze and the spontaneity of the moment rushing her into recklessness, she was forced to see the truth.

She wasn't brave at all. She was scared half to death. She was balancing on the edge of a cliff. Hanging on to the proverbial limb. About to tumble headlong into a relationship that came with only one guarantee: This man she was falling in love with was bent on walking away.

"It's not too late, Sara."

His voice was soft. His eyes were gentle. His words were one hundred percent wrong. It had been too late days ago. It had been too late the first time he held her in his arms and offered himself as a target for her hate so that she could quit beating up on herself.

"I'm a big girl, Tucker," she said, falling a little deeper in love because he'd nobly offered her another chance to back out. "I don't need you looking out for me. I need you making love to me."

He closed his eyes and swallowed. "You know that's where it ends."

It hurt. She'd expected it to. Still, she wasn't giving up on making his words a lie. She was banking on his desire outweighing his denial. Relying on the instincts that told her desire wasn't the only factor in this equation.

So she smiled, as an offer of assurance that she wouldn't cling, wouldn't cry, wouldn't fall apart when he decided it was over and done.

"What I know is that every time we seem to get started, something manages to stop us."

With a boldness that did her heart proud, she walked around him and unplugged the phone. "That's to make sure we see this through to the finish this time."

He smiled then. And shook his head. And pushed himself slowly away from the door.

With a hammering pulse, she watched him come to her. With a catch in her breath, she took the hand he extended. With her heart on the line, she followed him…then offered a puzzled smile when he didn't lead her to the bedroom.

"Has anyone ever suggested that your sense of direction may be a little skewed?" she asked as he tugged her back into the kitchen.

"If I recall, you said you'd do the dishes." His look told her that dishes were the last thing on his mind. "Besides, we have a little unfinished business to take care of in here."

"Business?" she repeated as her gaze followed his to the kitchen table. "Oh. *That* business."

His smile promised things to come. "All in good time." Then he rolled up his sleeves.

So, he wanted to play some more. That was fine. That was good. If that was all she could get from him tonight, she'd take it, no questions asked. It allowed him to think there was no threat of her getting too close. As illusions went, it was a simple one.

The question, still, was why he was so resistant? The question was, would he ever admit the truth? She knew it was possible that he would win the battle of wills. That bothered her more than anything else. What if his penchant for self-denial was stronger than her determination to convince him he deserved more?

Shaking off the fear, she pasted on a plucky smile and made herself live for the moment.

"There's something about the look of a man elbow-deep in soapsuds that does my heart good," she said a few minutes later as she stood beside him at the sink, a dish towel in her hand.

With a swift shift of his hand, he snagged her wrist and pulled her between him and the sink.

"And there's something about an ornery woman that brings out a vindictive streak in me." Crowding tight against her, he wedged her hips to his, making certain she felt his arousal against her tummy.

"Ornery?" She squeezed out the one word, gasping at the strength and size of him pressed against her. "Me?"

"Ornery. You," he assured her as he tugged her shirt from her jeans and lifted it over her head. "We won't be needing this."

She shivered and, feeling the delicious tug of decadence and danger, braced her elbows behind her on the lip of the sink. "Is this the part where the unfinished business comes in?"

"Umm-hmm..." With slow, deliberate movements, he unsnapped her bra.

"Tucker...it's broad daylight. What if..."

"What if what?" he asked in a low, husky murmur as he peeled the lace straps down her arms.

"What if T-Tag comes...back?"

"Then he can finish the dishes."

His smile was wicked and full of sin. "In the meantime, I can think of a hundred things I'd rather do with these bubbles."

She caught her bottom lip between her teeth when he dipped his hands in the water, then brought them to her breasts, his cupped palms full of warm water and bubbles.

Warm, callused hands covered her breasts with hot, soapy water and a gentle trail of bubbles that trickled down her midriff.

She sucked in a shuddering breath as wet heat slithered under the waistband of her jeans to arrow and pool low on her belly, where her body reacted to his erotic stimulation.

"Do...you think..." she whispered, getting lost in

the sensual swirl of air-cooled wet skin and Tucker's massaging hands. "Do you think there's a chance we should be worrying about this...this fixation we seem to have developed for w-water?" she finally managed on a breathy gasp.

He skimmed damp, spread palms down her hips, then under her thighs, and lifted her, urging her legs around his waist.

"No more than you should be worried about the consequences of playing your inventive game of footsie under the table."

With her arms twined around his neck and her ankles locked behind his back, he walked across the room. Hooking a chair leg with his foot, he dragged it out from under the table and, with her straddling his lap, sat down.

"All right, little cowboy," he purred as his broad hands skated up and down the length of her bare back, "you started something here a little earlier.... What I want to know is, how do you plan to finish it?"

"Plan?" She widened her eyes in innocence, loving his adventurous aggression, loving the feel of him beneath her and the promise that loving Tucker could be as playful as it was exciting. "I didn't have a plan."

A dare both menacing and suggestive darkened his eyes. "So make one."

She swallowed, then drew a deep breath. "Maybe...maybe you could give me some ideas."

He smiled, soft and sexy, and her heart turned to mush. He lifted a hand to her hair and smoothed it back from her eyes. "Here's an idea. One of us—" his gaze dropped heatedly to her bare breasts "—is overdressed. Now work with it."

She held his bold blue gaze as her fingers found their way to the snaps running down the length of his chest. "I see what you mean."

With more speed than finesse, she rectified the situation, popping open the snaps to reveal inch after glorious inch of tanned skin and toned muscle and a tantalizing trail of coarse chamois-colored curls arrowing downward toward his belt buckle.

He chuckled at her aggressive approach.

"You have a gorgeous chest, Tucker Lambert," she whispered after she'd peeled the shirt from his broad shoulders and helped him free his arms.

"I like yours better," he said with a lazy caress of his eyes. His hands rose to her breasts and cupped them. "It's prettier. And softer. Like velvet," he murmured, watching the play of his fingers across her skin.

His eyes lifted slumberously to hers when her nipples hardened. "You like that? What else do you like, Sara? Tell me."

She shivered and let her eyes drift shut. "Your mouth." It came out on a whisper that hummed with breathless anticipation.

"Open your eyes."

With a languor born of arousal, she obeyed.

"Show me where."

Her gaze lowered with heated expectancy to where

his hands caressed her before returning to his mouth and lingering.

He slowly shook his head. "Not good enough. Show me."

Swallowing hard, she raised her hands to cover his. With slow, deliberate movements, he released her, then clamped his fingers gently around her wrists.

"Show me," he repeated with a hot burn of his eyes, and guided her hands to her breasts.

Lost in his promise, helpless to deny him, she cupped them in her hands. As he watched. And waited. And made her touch the spot that ached for his mouth to suckle.

With a groan that relayed what her wanton request did to him, he bracketed her ribs with his hands and lowered his head.

She arched her back on a sigh and lifted her breast to his mouth, crying out when his impatient wet heat surrounded her. The dark stubble of his jaw scraped her skin with a sweetly savage friction as he claimed her with a hunger that drove her wild, then a gentleness that humbled her.

"Tucker," she pleaded, cradling his head in her hands and burying her face in his hair. "Please…take me to bed."

Wrapping her tightly against him, he rose. Kicking the chair out of his way, he carried her to his bedroom.

Her gaze went unerringly to the bed, then back to Tucker as he lowered her in a slow, stunning glide to the floor. The pulsing friction of their bodies sliding against each other heated skin and melted bone. She clung to him, needy and weak.

"Not exactly sunshine or soapsuds, but it should do," he whispered, as his big hands drifted in a sweeping, sensual glide from her bare shoulders to her waist.

Through a haze of longing, she sensed a sudden hesitancy in him that told her the game had taken on new meaning.

As hard as it was to believe, he was nervous with her. This man, who played at love, was suddenly very serious. And very uncertain of what it all meant.

Her smile was reassuring, her voice as soft as the blue of his eyes. "It'll do," she assured him, touching her fingers to his jaw. "And so will you."

She got lost in the look he gave her then, became immersed in the moment as he moved to the bed and sat down. With his hands still encompassing her waist, he tugged her between his spread thighs and pressed his face to her breast.

Thoughts of moments past, of women he'd had, of the life he'd lived, faded like bad dreams at sunrise when he drew her snug against him. In that moment, heat and anticipation, generosity and need, outdistanced even her own feelings of failure and fear.

All she felt was this man and the emotions he evoked in her. Tenderness and compassion. Desperation and desire. And the moment that was theirs. The moment that was now.

She cradled his head in her hands. Burying her fingers in his hair, she lowered her head to his and held him close as his warm breath fanned her flesh and made her shiver.

Unhurried in his exploration, uninhibited in his demands, he tugged down her zipper, then drew her jeans an inch at a time down her hips, his mouth ascending to the warm concave of her belly.

And she fell a little deeper in love.

She'd expected fast and furious. She'd have welcomed rough and ravaging. He gave her leisurely instead. He gave her the pleasure of slow heat and exquisite loving. In the reverent stroke of his hand at her throat. In the whispered encouragement for her to finish undressing him. In the lush, lazy journey of his mouth across her body when they finally lay naked on his bed.

Flesh to flesh, heartbeat to heartbeat, they came together. His strength a stunning contrast to her fragility. His sinew and his dark bulk a complement to her pliancy and her pale, slim limbs.

In his bed, she discovered a new reason for living. In his arms, she learned that physical love could be a spiritual experience. With clever hands and hungry mouth, he made love to her. With whispered words and gentle urgings, he taught her joy she'd never known.

And when she thought she'd experienced every sizzling sensation possible, he introduced her to yet another when he knelt between her thighs and lifted her hips to the tender enticement of his mouth.

She forgot he was a practiced lover. Didn't care that he was skilled in the finer points of the art. She only wanted what he was willing to give her. Only wanted him.

And wanted him...and wanted him until she clenched her fists in the tangled sheets and begged him. *"Please..."*

With a languor that made her whimper, he lifted his head. Resting his cheek against the inside of her thigh, he looked up the length of her body, one broad palm spread possessively over her belly.

His eyes glittered like a fallen angel's as he turned his mouth to the pale flesh of her thigh and placed a long, biting kiss there. When he raised his gaze to hers again, his golden hair, beautifully mussed from her own greedy hands, fell across his eyes, beckoning her to ask him again.

"Please..."

"Please what, Sara?"

She swallowed and reached for him. "Please come inside me."

Watching her face, he slid the flat of his palm down her belly, then slipped his fingers inside her.

"Like this?" he whispered as she groaned and moved against the sweet, sensual rhythm he set.

"Yesss... Noooo..."

He lowered his head to the dark curls where her pleasure point pulsed with anticipation.

"Like this?" he murmured, then slipped his tongue into her cleft and sent her over the razor edge of sensation, where pleasure flirted gloriously with pain.

She cried out and writhed against him, afraid she'd die if he stopped, certain she would if he didn't. She quit fighting him then…and let his will take over. Let him stroke and finesse and redefine the act of love as something she'd never known.

Only when she crested, in a shimmering rush of white-hot sensation that left her breathless and murmuring his name, did he rise above her. Only when she thought he'd wrung every nuance of pleasure from her trembling body did he roll on protection and come inside her.

Only then did she realize he'd just begun.

He filled her with a sleek, heavy glide that stole her will and her waning powers of thought. He pleased her with his strength and a rich, seductive rhythm that pulsed as vitally as her heartbeat, as necessary as each labored breath she drew.

Clinging, clawing, craving his heat and his weight and his wild, driving possession, she came again in a blinding climax of delirious sensation and intoxicating speed.

She cried his name, then held him tight, fiercely hanging on as he drove them a full foot up the bed with one final, profound thrust and an exultant, guttural cry.

Twilight whispered into the room, washing the walls with dusky darkness, painting misty shadows on the man lying beside her.

Sara stretched like a cat, then drew the sheet to her breasts as she propped her chin on her palm and watched him sleep. Even in slumber, he had a rakish, renegade look about him. Yet, even then, a vulnerability that belied both claims managed to bleed through.

Such a wild, passionate lover. Such a giving, generous man. He wasn't selfish, as he'd like her to believe. He'd taken such care with her. Such wondrous, exquisite care. A man who didn't want to become involved would have had sex with her. Tucker Lambert had made love. Not like a man skirting commitment. Not like a man determined not to care. Like a man who wanted everything a relationship between a man and a woman offered, but who was afraid to take for himself.

What made you so afraid of taking, Tucker Lambert? That niggling question haunted her as she let her gaze travel around the dimly lit room...a room that was furnished with only the barest of necessities. A bed. A dresser. A rack for his hat, an extra pair of boots on the floor. Spartan, sparse. It was a room that carried the marks of a man who put little value on creature comforts, and it added to her impression that he put even less value on himself.

"Redecorating?"

She smiled, letting her gaze drift back to see him awake and watching her. "Just wondering."

He turned on his side to face her, plumping a pillow under the arm that he folded beneath his cheek. "About?"

About how to reach you and wishing it wasn't so important that I do, she wanted to say. But it was too soon. And the moment was too special to risk losing. Still, there was an issue to settle that she didn't feel comfortable putting off—even if it meant it might bring an end to her night with him.

"About whether or not you want me to stay here tonight."

She'd hoped he wouldn't have to think about it. Yet, when hesitation momentarily clouded his eyes and had her mentally kicking herself for asking, she willed him to take a little more time.

She was holding her breath by the time he reached for her. He was watching her face as he pulled her close.

"You seem to be forgetting that appetite you worked so hard at building."

"Ah..." she said, feeling her smile spread into something warm and willing and wonderful. "That's right. It's coming back to me now. Something... something about taking all night to satisfy it."

He rolled to his back and pulled her over on top of him. Running his hands down the length of her spine, he skimmed her bottom, then caressed the back of her thighs.

"Paybacks are hell," he said, parting her thighs, then easing her over his heat.

"Oh, but you're wrong," she whispered, sinking down around him. "Paybacks are...heaven."

Then he proved it to her by taking her there.

Eight

"**D**amn, if you're not the biggest fool known to God, man or machine, Lambert," Tucker swore under his breath as he gathered the reins and fought to concentrate on the gelding's moves.

It was a losing battle, as his thoughts drifted back, against his will, to Sara.

One night, he'd told himself. He'd allow himself the luxury of keeping her with him for one night. That was his style. That was his speed.

That was the only option.

To even think about extending his time with her went against every promise he'd made to himself. If he'd had principles—which he obviously didn't, or he never would have taken her to his bed—it would have gone against them, too.

But she was such a sweet, giving woman. Such a willing, playful lover, that one night had stretched to two. Two to a week, and still he couldn't bring himself to let her go.

He'd broken every rule he'd ever made about involvement. Rules that forbade waking up with a woman in his bed. Rules that prohibited the kind of indulgence that led to expectations. He'd been feeding those expectations. He'd known from the outset that she thought she cared about him. That alone should have kept him away from her. Her daddy and the tangle they'd had in the past should have done it.

And still he hadn't made her go.

He told himself it was because he didn't want to hurt her. He told himself it had nothing to do with needs he hadn't known he harbored, a sense of peace he'd never thought he'd claim.

He lied.

His mount missed another lick. His fault. Again. He hadn't been paying close enough attention. Sara had become his habitual weakness.

With renewed determination, he gathered the laboring gelding beneath him and focused on the calf. When he picked up on the white-faced steer, he reined him in.

"Pretty impressive."

At the sound of Sara's voice, he had to will himself to check a smile. He eyed her from beneath his hat brim as he dismounted. Tugging off his gloves, he turned the gelding over to Tag to cool him down before he did any more damage.

Then he told himself he wasn't glad to see her.

"He's coming," he said, and walked toward the board fence, where she stood with a mug of coffee in each hand. "He's got an awful lot of cow smarts, good athletic bend and flex."

"I was talking about you, cowboy."

Avoiding her eyes, he thumbed back his hat, wiped the sweat from his brow with the back of his sleeve, and accepted the mug she offered.

"You're a natural," she added, smiling up at him over the rim of her mug.

He shrugged and gave up—as he always did—letting go of the smile she managed to coax out of him. "I'm a Texan."

"It's more than that," she insisted. "You're in love with it. It shows."

She had him there. Though he fought it, it pleased him that she understood. He hiked a boot on the lower fence rail and propped his forearms over the top rung. "I guess you could say it's gotten in my blood. Kind of like dust on a dry day. I can't get away from it. Truth is, I can't imagine ever wanting to."

She didn't say anything. She just looked at him with that soft smile that made him want to talk some more and gradually wore down his determination to resist doing just that.

"From the day I left home," he heard himself saying, "and got a job mucking stalls and doing most anything dirty and hard on a cutting-horse ranch, I've wanted to train cutters."

"When was that?" she asked, watching his face. "That you left home, I mean."

He worked his jaw. "When I was eighteen."

"Why so young?"

He drew a deep breath before answering, then surprised himself again, when he didn't whitewash the truth with a line of bull. "Economics. Mom had her hands full feeding herself and Tag. She didn't need me to add to the problem. So I left, got a job and sent money home."

He could see in her eyes that she was sorry about the hand fate had dealt him. He was sorry then that he hadn't sloughed off grim reality with a throwaway line. He didn't want her pity. He didn't want her admiration. He deserved neither one.

"Hell, I was ready to split anyway," he lied, painting the picture he wanted her to see. "There was a song out last year. Something about being born dirt poor and dreaming about growing up and getting out of the rut." He shrugged again. "That was me. All I wanted to do was leave. And I didn't care if I ever walked that dead-end country road again."

"Which explains why you came back and took care of your brother when your mother died," she said with a knowing look and a contrary tilt of her head.

"Don't go reading more into it. Somebody had to do it."

"*Somebody* didn't. *You* did. Why do you always sell yourself so short, Lambert? You didn't have to come back."

Uncomfortable with her probing eyes, he downed

a swallow of coffee, then tossed the dregs in the bottom of the mug into the dust. "Yeah, well, I was at loose ends, anyway."

She cocked her head. "Whatever you say," she said, but her look said she wasn't buying a bit of it.

"So, how's Lana doing this morning?" he asked, wanting to change the subject before she got him singing like a snitch in a bad cops-and-corruption movie.

"She's fine. In fact, she shooed me out of the kitchen and started breakfast. She sent me down here to make sure you and Tag get your 'skinny cowboy butts'—her words, not mine—to breakfast.

"It's not, you know," she added as he opened the gate and joined her on the other side.

"What's not?"

"Your butt. It's not skinny. In fact, as butts go— and I've poked needles in my share of them—it's a fairly fine butt. Actually, it's better than fine, it's—"

"Quiet, woman," he growled, giving up his resistance and hooking an arm around her neck. He tucked her close to his side. "Before that mouth gets you in trouble again."

Her mouth got her in trouble later that night. The sweetest kind of trouble he'd ever known.

Every time they came together, there was more fire, more frenzy, more wild, thrilling excitement that left them panting and weak. Tonight, though, there was even more...a new element to her lovemaking, an urgency she initiated that sent him over the edge to oblivion.

"Sweet Lord, Sara," he hissed through clenched teeth. Arching his neck, he knotted his hands in the silk of her hair and rode with the rhythm of her hot, hungry mouth surrounding him.

When he couldn't take any more, he cupped her head in his hands and lifted her. Dragging her up the length of his body, he held her in a crushing embrace, laboring to catch his breath. "You're going to kill me."

"Not what I had in mind," she murmured around a string of wet, biting kisses.

With a groan, he rolled her beneath him and entered her in one swift, electric plunge.

Then all he heard was her breathless cries and his own thundering heartbeat as he tangled his fists in her hair and filled her with deep, driving strokes.

He was a lost man. He couldn't get enough of her. Couldn't get deep enough. Couldn't get close enough to her heat or her scent or her total trust and wanton acceptance of anything he asked her to do.

When he exploded inside her, it was with a series of hard, hammering thrusts that splintered into a million shards of blinding pleasure and bled him dry of every thought but one: What would his world be like without her?

"How much longer did you say it would take?" Sara asked as she consulted the road map.

"Another hour or so," Tucker said, checking his rearview mirror and pulling into the passing lane.

She still wasn't sure how it had happened, exactly, but one day had shuffled into another until the weekend rolled around, and she was still at Blue Sky. Much to Karla's dismay.

"Sara," she'd lectured over the phone on Thursday night, "don't you think it's time you came back to Dallas?"

What she'd meant was "don't you think it's time you got away from Tucker?" but she'd been too smart or too sensitive to say it.

Yeah, it was probably time, Sara agreed as she cast a look across the cab of the pickup and covertly studied Tucker's profile. It was probably past time, but she just couldn't bring herself to give it up.

The bottom line was, she was in love with him. Hopelessly, helplessly and, in all likelihood, futilely. Yet he hadn't sent her away. And the whisper of hope that he'd return her love refused to die.

Which was why, when Tag asked her to go to a competition with Tucker in his place, she'd agreed. Besides, there was the very real issue of Tag and Lana to consider. Tag didn't feel comfortable leaving Lana to deal with the stock for the few days the competition would keep them away. Sara agreed that it wasn't wise. It would have been different if they'd gotten a wrangler hired to take over the chores and keep an eye on things. To date, they hadn't gotten a single call in response to their ad.

She suspected that was why Tucker hadn't put the

brakes on the idea of her going along. He, too, saw the necessity.

When they pulled into the show grounds an hour and a half later, she forgot about the whys and the whynots. She was too busy dealing with a rush of excitement.

"I didn't expect it to be such a big competition," she said, taking in the volume of fancy rigs and high-priced horseflesh being unloaded from various trailers.

"With a hundred-thousand-dollar purse on the line, they're guaranteed a good draw," he said, climbing out of the cab.

"One hundred thousand?" she exclaimed, scooting out her side, then walking to the back of the trailer with him. "I guess I've been away from competition too long. I'd forgotten what a hefty price came with success."

"Yeah, well..." He unlatched the end gate, then reached for a lead rope. "Let's hope we get a little piece of that pie."

It was like the hush before the rise of the curtain, the quiet before the main event. The five-thousand-seat arena was filled to capacity with the rich and the confident, the wannabes and the hopefuls. And all eyes were currently on the three-year-old bay gelding and the lean, Hollywood-gorgeous cowboy settled on his back.

Sara sucked in a deep breath, her gaze straying for

a glimpse of the clock before returning to Tucker and the bay. Two and a half minutes to glory—or defeat.

It was the final round of competition after a three-day culling in which the cream of the entrants had risen to the top. Mason's black had been inched out in the semifinals by half a point. Still, she knew Tucker had been pleased by the little mare's performance, not having expected that good a showing. If she hadn't been injured last fall, she'd have been a great futurity prospect last winter. As a three-year-old, coming four, she still had a fine future ahead of her.

The bay was a different story. He'd consistently placed in the top ten in last year's futurity events. This year he was a mature horse, and Tucker had high expectations for him. He wasn't letting him down. The bay had smoked the competition going into the semifinal round, and now he had a chance to show what he was really made of.

Sara inched to the edge of her seat as horse and rider made a deep cut into the herd, moving with patience and practiced precision so as not to spook the milling Herefords.

The bay was on and he knew it. His wide, intelligent eyes were watchful, his fox ears forward and alert.

With a sureness that made it look easy, Tucker guided the gelding with the subtle touch of a knee, the barest pressure on the snaffle, until the calf he'd selected broke at a slow trot from the huddled throng.

The crowd murmured their quiet approval. Sara

drew a deep breath and wrapped her fingers in a death grip around the rail in front of her. In the speed of a camera flash, the action began.

With one hand on the horn, the other dropped low to allow complete, free rein, Tucker let the gelding have his head. It was up to the horse now. All the months of training and preparation for this moment had come to this. All he could do was hang on for the ride.

The audience went wild at the first move the gelding played against the calf. A roar of approval erupted like gunfire through the packed arena.

With her heart thundering in her throat, Sara got lost in the beauty and the art of man and animal cutting and dodging and "gettin' ground" in perfect harmony and with athletic grace. For the next two and a half minutes, the shouts and whistles sounding around her bled into the background as she surrounded herself with an acute awareness of only Tucker and the gelding and the calf.

When it was over and the arena was roaring with approval for a job well done, she pried her fingers from around the rail and waited for the score. It was 219. Again the crowd whistled and hooted and the arena resounded with applause when the fantastic score flashed on the board.

"Yes!" she whispered, and on shaking legs rose and went to meet Tucker behind the pens and wait for the final competitors to perform.

They'd settled for second, losing out to the dazzling performance of a seasoned veteran. Tucker was still extolling the virtues of both horse and rider over a thick steak two hours later.

"That old fox Murdock's still got a few tricks up his sleeve. And that old stud has seen more competitions than I've seen horses. Damn, they were something tonight."

Sara watched him across the table, slowly letting go of her disappointment as he dug into his T-bone. He was still fired up on adrenaline, flying high and fairly bouncing with afterburn energy.

"You're taking this better than I am," she sputtered, playing her fork through her salad.

"Darlin', eleven grand for second place makes for a heap of consoling. And if we had to lose, nothing could have been better than losing to that horse. Poco's his own son. His *own* son," he repeated meaningfully. "That old stud threw mostly fillies, and of the horse colts he did sire, most of them have been gelded or ended up reining horses or competing in pleasure classes. Poco's one of only two stud colts out of the old boy who are cutters. The other one's in Oklahoma, racking up points and prize money and twenty-five-hundred-dollar stud fees.

"When I enter Poco in the futurity in Fort Worth this winter, all eyes are going to be on that little stud of mine. If he rises to the occasion like his daddy, we'll have to build a new facility just to handle the ladies they'll be bringing to him to settle."

He grinned at her, then polished off his steak. "The

money from his stud fees alone will float the note on the spread.''

"And is Poco as good as his daddy?'' she asked, falling victim to that smile and his enthusiasm.

He sat back in his chair, looking smug and dangerous and utterly irresistible. "Does a cowboy ride with his boots on?''

They celebrated until midnight. In boots and jeans and high-flying spirits, they found a local night spot where the band was fine and the mood infectious. They Texas two-stepped, boot-scooted and slow-danced until the lazy, sensual rhythm of the music and their brushing bodies sent them sauntering to the truck in each other's arms.

Sara told herself it didn't matter how she felt when she saw how other women looked at Tucker. He'd turn heads dressed in a polyester leisure suit. He'd turn heads with a sack over his.

She told herself he was with her, and if there was never another moment than now, she wouldn't be sorry for the chance she'd taken.

Snuggled against him in the front seat of the truck, with the lights from the oncoming traffic flashing strobelike across the angular beauty of his face, she told herself all was right with her world—just before the world exploded in front of her eyes.

Tucker swore loudly as he hit the brakes and veered sharply left to avoid the wildly careering car in front of them.

The pickup fishtailed with a screech of tires and

complaining horsepower. Thanks to modern engineering and Tucker's skill behind the wheel, they kept the truck under control and squeezed past the troubled vehicle. Pulling to a skidding stop in the breakdown lane, they watched with horror as the car flipped end over end. After an excruciating, suspended eternity, the little compact landed on its hood in the center of the median, its wheels spinning drunkenly as it wobbled, then stilled.

"You okay?" Tucker asked, with a scowl as dark as the night.

"Fine. Fine," she repeated in a shaky whisper. "What happened?"

"I don't know." He looked over his shoulder at the wreckage behind them as he unbuckled his belt and shoved open the door. "Blowout, I think."

"Tucker, no!" she screamed when he bolted toward the wrecked car. "Tucker, stop! It could blow any minute."

If he heard her, he didn't care. And he sure as the world didn't listen. Propelled from her shock and fear, she scrambled out of the truck as he ran toward the car.

The older-model compact lay crumpled on its roof. Smoke poured from under the hood. The steel belly of the chassis gleamed under a vapor light, the skewed angle of a broken headlight gouging an eerie, fractured path of hazy light and murky shadows into the grassy median.

Her heart, already jackhammering, kicked up to an aching, exploding pressure when she smelled the om-

inous fumes of gasoline—then saw the glittering trail
of oily liquid running from the rear of the car to snake
along the highway.

"Tucker!" she screamed, as a fear as cloying as
the stench of death paralyzed her. "The gas tank's
leaking!"

He was beyond reason. He was on his back by the
driver's door, his feet braced against the frame for
leverage as he tugged like a man possessed on the
jammed door.

She felt as if she were watching from afar. Like a
drifter passing through a surreal nightmare over which
she had neither ownership nor control. Hours passed.
In reality, it was mere seconds, until she heard the
creak of complaining steel and the door gave way.

"Hurry!" she whispered, frozen to the pavement
like a post, knowing she should be helping, helpless
to make herself move.

Until he dragged the limp, bloody body from the
twisted death trap and carried it a safe distance from
the wreckage to the grass on the median. He was still
hovering over the lifeless mass of humanity when the
car blew, rocking the night with its fury, lighting the
dark with its rage.

She quit feeling then, as old instincts, victimized
by experience, prompted by duty, kicked into over-
drive and took control. Rushing to Tucker's side, she
made a quick, perfunctory check of vital signs, then,
sitting back on her heels, stripped the belt from her
jeans to use as a tourniquet.

Somewhere in the midst of the blood and broken

bones and carnage, a heart beat. Somewhere behind the closed eyelids and mangled skin, a life clung. A life she was determined to save.

She was peripherally aware of activity around her. Aware of Tucker shouting at a stopping motorist to call an ambulance on his car phone. Aware of the serrated scream of a distant siren.

Aware of Tucker by her side, responding quickly and surely to the orders she gave him, of his calming, steady presence when she sat back, exhausted, not knowing if she'd done all she could do.

Tucker was worried about her. She'd been deathly quiet since they'd watched the ambulance pull away. Deathly quiet and deathly pale when he asked her what she thought the chances of survival were.

Her eyes vacant, her voice drained of emotion, she'd only stared after the speeding ambulance, blood soaking her hands, smeared in her hair, staining her shirt and jeans.

"Fifty-fifty," she'd said, then turned away, walking like an ancient, haggard soul to the truck.

She hadn't spoken since. She'd climbed silently from the truck, stood aside as he fit the key in their motel room door, then walked on stiff, leaden legs to the shower.

Tucker had long since stripped off his shirt and jeans. With repeated glances toward the closed door, he'd washed the worst of the blood and dirt from his hands in the sink outside the bathroom. Behind the door, there was silence except for the steady drone of the shower spray.

He glanced at his watch. She'd been in there almost an hour. And he couldn't stand to wait outside another minute.

He gave the door a light rap with the back of his knuckle. "Sara."

No response.

"Sara," he repeated, louder this time, as every nerve in his body hummed with anxious expectancy.

When he was met by more silence, he gave the doorknob a try, then let out a relieved breath when it opened for him.

The bathroom was drenched in rolling steam, and the shower spray was still hissing. A dozen torn, empty soap wrappers littered the pile of bloody, discarded clothes that lay in a tangled heap on the white tile floor.

Then he saw her. She turned to him, water streaming over her body, her eyes haunted, her hands scrubbing and scrubbing and scrubbing, her skin red and raw.

His heart ricocheted in his chest, splintering into a million crumbling pieces.

"Sara." His voice was a mere whisper that relayed every heartfelt, heavy fear he had for her.

"It won't come off," she whispered, her eyes full of horror and appeal and plea as she looked from him to her hands and back to him again. "The blood. It won't come off. It never c-comes o-off."

He swallowed back a groan of anguish and went

to her. Hurting for her. Aching for her. Feeling, at this moment, that if he could, he would bleed and die for her.

He'd never seen eyes so haunted. Never seen panic so stark. And he knew then the depth of the problem that had brought her to Blue Sky.

"Can I help you?" he asked softly as he moved on instinct to her side. "Can I help you wash it off?"

"Yes…" she whispered fiercely, a glimmer of wild hope flashing in her eyes. "Help me. Help…me."

He caught her in his arms as she dissolved in a keening cry and crumpled to her knees in the tub.

With a care he'd never known he'd mastered, he took the soap bar from her hands. With a patience he forced himself to maintain, he bathed her trembling limbs, soothing, massaging, doing some trembling of his own.

She didn't protest when he turned off the shower. Didn't so much as whimper when he wrapped her in a towel and carried her to the bed.

Didn't close her eyes as he lay down beside her, shivering and distant and, in spite of his arms wrapped around her, totally, chillingly, alone.

Only when the minutes had stretched to another hour did he feel brave enough to try to reach her. He lifted his hand and let it fall lightly to her hair.

"Better now?" His whisper, laced with concern, was a gruff sound in the dimly lit room.

Silence, interrupted only by her shallow, tremulous breaths, filled the space between them.

"Sara…" The bed shifted as a latent rush of adrenaline brought him up on an elbow. "Sara, please. It's over. Please. Tell me you're okay."

"I didn't want to help," she whispered, turning guilt-filled eyes to his. "I didn't want to touch any more blood."

Then she rolled away from him, curling into herself, tucking into a small, tight ball.

Something raw and deep-reaching settled in his chest and made it ache. Only when he dropped a hand to the curve of her waist and she pulled away from him did he recognize it as fear.

After a desperate hesitation, he gathered her in his arms and drew her close, even as she fought him. Then she clung to him, as if he were her only anchor in an endless ocean of misery.

She let the tears fall then. In the dark, with the horror of the accident within touching distance, and the horror of all she'd seen in her career too close to bear, she let down her defenses and let the pain seep out.

She'd come to Blue Sky wounded. She'd come to Blue Sky to heal. She'd come to him a woman with oppressive control of her emotions, in total denial that she was bleeding and dying inside.

She wasn't in control any longer. She was letting go. And it was tearing her apart.

Her tears came in a flood, an endless river of wretched anguish that racked her fragile body until he feared she would shatter in his arms. He'd never felt so helpless in his life. Or so utterly embroiled in another person's pain.

He didn't press her to talk to him. He simply let her cry. He held her, and soothed her, and brushed the hair from her face. And when the worst was over, and her continued silence shut him out, he felt a loneliness unlike any he'd ever known.

He'd never wanted to be a part of her life. Yet he'd never wanted anything more than in this moment. He needed her to confide in him. He needed to fully understand the power of her demons. Instead, he got a better understanding of his own when her inability to let him help her cut to the bone and twisted.

Finally, exhausted, she slept. As he held her. As he hurt for her. As he lay awake through the night and wondered when he'd been so foolish as to let himself care. Wondering when he'd let himself fall in love with a woman whose soul was as wounded as his own.

Sara awoke to the strong daylight and an empty bed. Through swollen eyelids, she focused on the clock. Ten a.m.

She felt as if she'd slept for an eternity. She wished she could sleep for another. But she knew she had to get up.

With more will than strength, she rolled back the covers and stumbled to the bathroom. Every sign of last night's wreckage was gone. Tucker, she thought, his consideration tugging at her heart.

By the time she'd showered and dressed, she was feeling almost human. Would have felt cleansed if she could have dealt completely with the catharsis that had assaulted her last night with the violence of a bloodletting.

She hadn't known how deep the wounds were buried. Hadn't believed she harbored so much horror. Wasn't sure she had a handle on it yet. Deep down, she was afraid she never would.

She was running a brush through her hair when she heard Tucker slip the key into the lock and come into the motel room. Drawing a deep breath, she walked out of the bathroom to face him.

"How are you feeling?" he asked, searching her face with blue eyes that looked haggard with fatigue and concern.

"Embarrassed," she said, lowering her head.

He didn't say anything. Just touched a hand to her hair, then offered her coffee from a paper cup.

"Thanks." She took a long sip, then forced a smile. "This really helps. I'm feeling better already."

If feeling raw and exposed and as if her heart were bleeding was feeling better.

"She's going to make it," he said, watching her closely.

Her shoulders stiffened, but she couldn't say anything.

"I called the hospital, Sara. She's going to make it."

She pinched her lips together and nodded, feeling a compulsive urge to run away from the compassion in his eyes. He didn't understand. She didn't deserve his compassion. She didn't deserve his care.

Setting the paper cup on the dresser with a trembling hand, she mumbled something about needing some fresh air.

Slipping dark glasses over her eyes, she stepped out of the motel room. The sunlight was blinding. The air was already oppressively hot. But she had to get away from him.

She couldn't bear to see the concern in his eyes. Couldn't stand to look closer to see if maybe he did understand after all and his concern was struggling with disappointment.

He had every right to be disappointed. He'd been so wonderful last night. And she, who had been praying he'd open up and talk to her, had turned away from him when he asked the same of her. She'd tightened up like a clam and denied him the only thing he'd ever asked her to give him. An explanation.

Pinching her eyes shut, she fought a fresh onslaught of hot, burning tears.

His hand on her shoulder brought her head up.

"Sara…" he said, turning her toward him. He searched her face, trying to read the expression hidden behind her dark glasses. Whether he realized she was hiding or just didn't have it in him to push her, she'd never know. But the question he'd been going to ask never came.

Instead, he squeezed her shoulders with a gentle reassurance, then looked past her toward the truck. "It's time we load up and go home."

She wished she had the courage to talk to him. Instead, she was grateful that he'd backed away. Without a word, she went back to the room to pack her bag, aware of him watching her, aware of the hurt in his eyes.

More than anything, she was aware of her own fear. She was afraid to share with him what had happened to her last night. Afraid to expose her greatest weakness.

What twisted, ugly irony, she thought in grim silence. She'd always thought *he* was the one who was afraid to commit, yet when push came to shove, she was the one holding back.

Nine

They drove back to the stock barns and loaded the horses with silent competence, working together as they'd grown accustomed to doing over the past several days. When they were ready to head for Blue Sky, Sara made the perfunctory offer to drive. He gave the requisite decline and suggested she get some sleep.

So she sat beside him in the cab, pretending she was sleeping, letting him pretend he didn't know she wasn't.

The distance she erected with her silence lengthened with every mile they traveled. She just couldn't bring herself to talk about what had happened last night. She couldn't let herself tell him what she was feeling, just as he couldn't bring himself to ask.

The days that followed at Blue Sky were more of the same. Something that should have drawn them closer together had fallen like a wedge and was driving them further apart. On the surface, everything appeared fine. They worked together. Sometimes they even laughed together. They engaged in polite generalities and mundane conversation with Lana and Tag. But they never talked about the things that mattered. Not the past. Not the future. Not the lack of sharing that got in the way of the present.

The only level they could truly communicate on was physical. When he took her to his bed at night and made love to her, it was with a gentleness that was healing in itself, yet painful because it was bittersweet.

With the moon peeking in through the window and the night breeze rustling the curtains by the bed, he'd whisper his care through his kisses, tell her his regrets with his eyes.

Tender and slow, luxuriously sheltered, she'd rock in the harbor of his body and ride with the wonder of his touch.

Each night, when it was over and she lay snug in the pocket of his shoulder, she knew she should confide in him. Still, she couldn't bring herself to share more than the silence. She'd stare into the dark and wish she had the courage to tell him, wish she was convinced he wanted to know. But she was afraid to do it, afraid of how he would react. And not knowing was more comfortable than risking the probable truth.

Inevitably, she'd fall asleep with the ultimate question hovering: *If this was as good as they could give each other, how much more time would pass until what they did have came to an end?*

She didn't have to wonder long. The morning of the fifth day marked the beginning of that end.

The day's work was done. Lana was preparing supper while Sara sat out on the veranda, keeping Cody out of his mother's hair. Nestled in the shade of a cypress and the scent and color of Lana's crepe myrtle, she was enjoying Cody's antics when a truck pulled into the drive. With a squeal of brakes and the shuddering idle of a poorly running engine, the motor died with a cough and a wheeze.

Shading her eyes against the late-afternoon sun's glare, she rose with Cody on her hip and squinted through the dust at the rusted-out body and then at the man climbing out of the cab.

She decided almost immediately that he wasn't a client. The men and women who engaged Tucker in the training and showing of their horses were an affluent lot. This man, as evidenced by his truck, at least, couldn't have raised the price of a horse, let alone the cost of boarding and training one.

Yet there was something about him—the way he carried himself, with a cocky sort of confidence and a swagger that spoke of surety—that made her wonder if the aged truck might be an eccentricity rather than a necessity.

He paused and looked around him with the air of a man coming home. Hands on his slender hips, his features shaded by the brim of a Resistol, he took in Blue Sky, from the barns to the bunkhouse, to the guest casas and finally the ranch house. When he spotted her watching him, his mouth tipped up into a slow, well-well-what-have-we-here grin.

Sara felt an unaccountable stirring of unease skitter through her blood as he drew nearer and she got a closer look. He was a handsome man. His age was a hard call. The deep smile lines on either side of his eyes and the streaks of silver threaded through the chamois-colored hair at his temples suggested early-to-mid-fifties. His stature and build—tall and lean and still firmly muscled—suggested a decade less.

His dress denims had seen some wear, as had his calfskin boots. Both were clean and neat, as was the fawn-colored Resistol he wore at an angle that was both flirty and fashionable.

Shifting Cody's weight a little higher on her hip, she glanced toward the door, expecting to see Tucker or Tag slip outside to investigate. When neither did, she walked to the archway to get a better look—and froze. Her heart stalled in her throat when she saw his face clearly and connected with the heartbreak blue of his eyes.

"Evenin', pretty lady," he said with an appreciative smile as he sized her up, tipped his hat, then settled it back on his head. "Never expected to see a delicate little thing like you stuck out here in the middle of nowhere. Makes a man wonder what that boy of mine could be thinking. But then again, maybe I understand after all. If I had me a fine little filly like you, I believe I'd be hiding you away out in the boonies, myself. Yes, ma'am. I believe I would.''

Her heart sank when his words cemented what her eyes had convinced her was true. He wasn't just a man. He was John Lambert. Tucker and Tag's father.

This was the man who brought the dark look to Tucker's eyes and whose name she'd never heard Tag mention. As she looked at him, stunned by the physical similarities his sons bore to him, she was equally shaken by the contrast in manner.

While Tucker and Tag both exuded unconscious sexuality and self-confidence, this man forced both issues. On him, it was distasteful and obviously overdone.

"Tuck around?" he asked as he skimmed her body again with his bold stare, then flicked his gaze to the door when it opened behind her.

Sara turned to see Tucker step out onto the brick-colored tile of the veranda. His face was a mask of jumbled emotions—none of which was affection.

"Hey, boy," John Lambert said, smiling as if he expected an open-arms welcome.

"You lost, old man?" Tucker's voice, like his face, was as hard as granite.

The elder Lambert cocked his head, the wattage of his smile barely fading. "Hell, no, I ain't lost. I know exactly where I am. And thanks to this—" he held up a dog-eared newspaper want-ad section "—now I know where you are, too.

"Son of a gun, boy, you've done all right for yourself," he said with an expansive look around as he tucked the ragged piece of newsprint into his chest pocket. "All right, indeed," he added, with a smug grin that he tried to pull off as pride but that Sara thought looked more like greed.

"What do you want?" Tucker asked flatly.

Sara's gaze shot back to Tucker. His eyes were a cool gunmetal blue, as accusing as a prosecutor bent on conviction.

"What do I want?" John Lambert repeated with an incredulous sigh. "What do I *want?* That's all you've got to say to your daddy after all these years?"

"What did you want me to say?" Tucker's expression never altered. "That I was glad to see you?"

"And why the hell not?" Lambert returned with a good-ol'-boy grin as he walked closer to his son. Hands on his hips, he shook his head. "Still the same old hothead, ain'tcha? Thought maybe time woulda mellowed you some, boy. Lord knows, if I had a spread like this and a woman like her—" he tossed a smile full of innuendo toward Sara "—I believe I'd be a real mellow fellow."

"You had a woman," Tucker said in a dangerously soft voice.

The older Lambert had the decency to look shamed. "That I did. That I did," he repeated, with a grim set to his mouth. "And I hope you're smarter than me, who didn't know a good thing when he had it."

Tucker didn't so much as move an eyelash, yet Sara could sense a rage building, as sure as the sun was setting. Any minute now she expected him to act on that rage. And while she might have felt like rooting him on, she couldn't see any good coming from physical violence.

"I'm Sara Stewart," she said, stepping between Tucker and his father. "I'm a friend of Tucker's."

"Stewart?" John Lambert's gaze swept her again in a suggestive way that she knew would set Tucker off if she didn't do something to stop it. "My pleasure, Miz Stewart," he added, with an emphasis on her last name and a look at Tucker that made her uncomfortable.

"And this is your grandson," she added quickly, shifting Cody on her hip. "Cody is Tag and Lana's boy."

"Lana?" The elder Lambert reached for the bouncing two-year-old, then laughed when Cody tugged his hat down over his eyes.

"Tag's wife," Tucker interjected darkly. "Something you would have known if you'd ever bothered to check."

"Well, hell, son…that's what I'm doing now. I'm checkin'. Never figured I'd find both my boys here, though. And a grandson to boot. Guess I hit the jackpot."

Tucker felt like hitting something. The jackpot didn't come to mind.

He'd felt like he'd been thrown from a Brahma when he stepped outside and saw his father standing there. It had been eight years. And it hadn't been long enough.

Anger, humiliation and resentment all tunneled into one burning knot in his gut as he watched him. But hate was the strongest emotion of them all. Hate for the father who'd never been there. Hate for the child within who still clung to that scrap of need to please and forgive and even love this man he couldn't ever remember calling Daddy. The man who'd never been there for him or for Tag or for their mother.

The last time he'd seen John Lambert had been the day after he buried her. The bastard hadn't even had it in him to make it to the funeral, pleading business or a big deal or whatever bull he felt like spreading that particular day. On the list of John Lambert's sins, that was at the top, higher than all the grief he'd caused Tucker's mother. Higher even than the "Hey, what would *I* do with a fourteen-year-old kid?" response when he'd blown out of town, leaving Tag with Tucker. Higher than the legacy the old bastard had given him.

"You're a big one, ain'tcha boy?" Lambert said with a grin as he hefted Cody against him. "Musta got them eyes from your mama though, 'cause they sure ain't Lambert eyes."

Another pair of Lambert eyes looked through the screen at that moment. After a long look, Tag stepped outside.

"Well, look at you," John Lambert said when Tag, as hesitant as Sara had ever seen him, joined them on the veranda. "Last time I saw you, you were about as meaty as a lone wolf, and just as mean."

Tag looked from his father to Tucker, solemn and confused.

"It seems our *daddy*," Tucker began, his eyes never leaving his father's, "decided it was time to check on us. Loving father that he is, he just couldn't stay away another eight years."

Lambert shook his head, his smile unshakable. "Still got a mouth on you boy. Y'all just get pissy-mad if you want to, but we both know you never needed me around, anyway. Hell, as a matter of fact, looks like you did just fine all on your own. Here, take this little critter, will ya, son? I've wrestled smaller steers than him. He's about to break my arm."

Tag reached for Cody just as Lana burst out the door.

"What's going...on?" she asked, her voice trailing off when she saw Tucker's dark glare, Tag's look of haunted yearning, and the man whose eyes they shared.

"Well," Lambert said, his gaze skimming Lana's dark beauty and lush curves. "My boys sure do know how to pick 'em. You must be Lana," he added, before his appreciation for his son's wife became too obvious. "Pleased to meet you, missus. Mighty proud to be your daddy-in-law. And I'll be forever grateful that you made this lonesome old man a grandpa."

Tucker wanted to swing at him. If not for all his past transgressions, for showing up at his home and flashing all that South Texas charm and homespun cock-and-bull.

He decided to settle for showing him back to his beat-up truck. Until he saw the look on Tag's face.

He closed his eyes and swore under his breath. Damn you, John Lambert. Damn you for coming here, stirring up old hurts and reminding Tag he had a father. He'd needed and missed his father, and was still young enough to wonder if there was anything in his daddy worth latching on to.

"What brings you to Blue Sky?" Tag asked, trying to sound like a man, not the child who had wondered about and waited for his father to come home.

The older man's attention swung to his youngest son. "Why, you did, son. You and your brother." His gaze strayed then to Tucker, all the swagger and sureness leaving his face. "I admit I wasn't much of a husband to your mama. Wasn't much of a daddy to you boys. It's too late to make it up to your mother, and for that I'll always be sorry. But I'd like to give it another try with you. Figured maybe, man to man, we just might make it work."

Just as Sara had moved without comment or fuss into the ranch house with Tucker, John Lambert moved into the little guest casa she had vacated.

Just as Sara hurt for Tucker in silence, Tucker bore his anger with a clench-jawed determination to keep it in check.

It took Sara until the fifth night to work up her courage and ask, "Do you want to talk about it?"

They were in bed. They hadn't made love since his father had been here. Each night that passed, she felt

Tucker slipping further away. The look in his eyes just before he rolled onto his side and away from her made her realize just how vast that distance had grown.

"Tucker?" she said softly, needing to open some line of communication.

"You don't really want to hear what I've got to say." His voice was heavy with the weight of years of disappointment and disillusionment.

"Maybe he's changed," she suggested hopefully.

He snorted and punched the pillow. "Skunks don't change their stripes, darlin'. John Lambert hasn't changed his ways."

"He seems genuinely interested in Tag."

A long silence followed before he turned back to her. Flicking on the light, he propped himself on an elbow, his eyes as hard as crystal as he loomed over her.

"Get this through your head, Sara. The only thing genuine about John Lambert is his past performance. He doesn't care about that boy. He cares about himself. To get what he wants, he'll make you believe anything."

When she frowned at his cynical words, he dragged a hand through his hair.

"He's at his best when he has an audience, all right? Tag is like playing to a new crowd. He doesn't have enough memories to form an opinion, good or bad. He wants so badly for the old man to be his daddy, he's tripping over himself to please him, and he's playing right into his hand.

"And you want to know where that leaves me? That leaves me standing back and watching it, knowing that when our *daddy* finally comes clean with the real reason he's here, it's going to knock the props out from under Tag and I'm going to be left picking up the pieces when he falls. Me and Lana."

He closed his eyes, then let out a deep breath. There was such anger, such hurt, in him that she knew she couldn't dispel it.

"Then why did you let him stay?"

"Do you really think I had a choice?"

No, she realized. He hadn't. If he had made John leave, it would have left Tag resentful and full of regret. That resentment would have been aimed at Tucker. The regret could have grown into anger. Again, Tucker would have borne the brunt of it.

"What are you going to do?" she asked softly.

He looked past her to the shadows dancing on the walls.

"Wait," he said finally. "Wait for him to show his hand."

Then he turned off the light and turned away. Again.

She laid a hand on his shoulder.

"Go to sleep, Sara," he said, rebuffing her offer of comfort with a heavy sigh.

But she didn't sleep. Not for a very long time.

"You're giving him too much head, son. That martingale's way too loose. And you ought to be using a snaffle instead of that side pull. He ain't never gonna get good ground if you don't show him who's boss.''

Sara watched astride Jezibel as John Lambert shouted a string of orders to Tag, who was working a little red roan gelding. Tucker observed it all with a dangerous set to his jaw.

It hadn't started out this way. At first John had been content to sit back, express his approval and, to all appearances, feel pride in his sons' accomplishments. Little by little, though, he'd started adding his opinions. Expressing his views. Subtly undercutting Tucker's authority and questioning his judgment. Today, he wasn't being so subtle. And Tucker had had enough.

With a casualness that concealed his agitation, Tucker kneed his mount and rode slowly over to where his father stood by the fence.

''I'd appreciate it if you'd leave the training to us.'' His voice was deceptively quiet.

''Well, boy, I'd like to,'' Lambert said, a smug, authoritative look on his face, ''but it appears to me that you could use my advice on this particular colt. He's too headstrong.''

''What he is, is a bit shy, and it comes across as stubborn,'' Tucker explained, with a patience Sara hadn't thought was in him. ''He needs a real light hand and a long look at a calf to build his confidence.''

Unspoken was the ''And I don't need you undermining my methods.''

The older Lambert made a show of lifting his hands

in supplication. ''Whatever you say, boy. I was just trying to help.''

With a look that said, ''Yeah, sure you were,'' Tucker turned his mount back to Tag and the workout. And Tag, as usual, was caught in the middle wanting to please the only man who had ever looked out for him, wanting to win the favor of the man who never had.

The sun was setting low against a backdrop of rust-red sky and a parchment-paper horizon when Sara slipped outside. She needed some time to herself. She had some thinking to do. Thinking wasn't something that came easy in the Lambert household these days.

The tension around the supper table was thicker than sludge. Tucker was stone-faced and silent. John was talkative and full of fatherly wit and grandfatherly advice. Tag was caught somewhere between them. Sara knew he wanted to believe in his father, yet he couldn't discount his brother's resentment of the man. She hurt for both of them. But, mostly, she hurt for herself.

John Lambert's appearance at Blue Sky had served to lengthen the distance between her and Tucker. Before he'd come, they'd been walking a precarious wire between hanging on and letting go. Since he'd arrived, letting go seemed the only option. Tucker had closed himself off from her completely.

It wasn't that she hadn't known up front, she reminded herself. It wasn't as if he hadn't warned her he didn't have anything to give a relationship. Relationship? She wrapped her arms around the adobe arch of the courtyard and sagged against it. There had never been a relationship. There had been tentative friendship and delirious sex. Now, there wasn't even that.

"That's an awful sad face for such a pretty little girl."

Sara straightened slowly at the sound of John Lambert's voice. She turned to face him as he sauntered toward her.

"Just enjoying the sunset," she lied.

He smiled. "Right. Just like my oldest son is enjoying my visit. I don't understand that boy," he said, walking up beside her. "I guess I understand why he doesn't want me around, but I don't understand why he's taking it out on you."

She didn't want to talk to him about Tucker. In fact, she didn't want to talk to him at all. She forced a tight smile and made to step around him. "I guess I'll go in now. It's been a long day."

His hand on her arm stopped her. His grip was both imprisoning and familiar. Far too familiar, as he ran his thumb in a slow caress along her arm. "You don't have to run from me, Sara. And you don't have to put up with that silent treatment Tucker's been dishing out. One thing I know how to do is make a lady forget her problems."

Her eyes flashed to his. She didn't want to believe what she'd just heard. When she saw the dark spark of sexual interest in his eyes, however, she knew she hadn't misunderstood.

Revulsion and disgust rolled in her stomach. "Please let go of my arm."

"Now, Sara," he said soothingly, moving closer when she tried to pull away. "No need to be that way."

"Get the hell away from her."

Sara's head snapped around at the sound of Tucker's voice. The stark, unharnessed rage in his words split the air like a bullet as his tall dark form emerged from the shadows of the covered courtyard.

With a slow, deliberate show of good-natured acquiescence, John released her arm and turned toward his son, a nasty smile tilting his mouth. "Just trying to spread a little goodwill, boy. 'Course, that's something you wouldn't know nothing about, would you?"

Tucker's eyes darkened with a dangerousness that frightened Sara.

"Get off my ranch."

"You know," John said, propping his fists on his hips, "I've just about lost my patience with you. There's something you seem to have forgotten, boy. I'm your daddy. I deserve a little respect."

"You deserve? You *deserve?*" Tucker repeated, in a tone that seethed with bitter cynicism. "What you deserve has nothing to do with respect."

Lambert turned to Sara, his eyes full of mocking appeal. "Listen to him, would you? Mr. High-and-Mighty. Such a flawless, respectable example." He was baiting Tucker now, his good-ol'-boy facade finally breaking. "I suppose you think you deserve better? Well, maybe we ought to ask your little brother what he thinks you deserve. He thinks the damn sun rises and sets on your miserable carcass.'' Venom soured his words, making Sara cringe.

"Better yet, let's ask little Sara what she thinks, eh, boy?'' He turned blue eyes glittering with vindictiveness to Sara. "What do you think, Sara? Do you think a man who plays around with his boss's wife deserves any more respect than a man who's simply trying to lend a supporting shoulder to his son's current lover?''

Tucker's fist came out of nowhere. The crack of knuckle connecting with bone made a sickening sound in the still Texas night. John Lambert slammed against the adobe arch, then sagged to the ground.

Shaking his head to clear it, Lambert spit blood, then wiped his mouth with the back of his hand. "What's the matter boy? Don't the tale set too well when the nasty little story's about you?''

Sara watched, unable to move, as Tucker loomed over his father. Latching on to him with a two-fisted grab of his shirtfront, he dragged him to his feet.

"What's it going to take to get you out of here?'' he snarled between clenched teeth.

The older Lambert eyed his son with an ugly, victorious sneer. "And I thought you'd never ask.

"I want Tag,'' he said with hostile indifference, then smiled when he saw Tucker's stunned expression. "I want to be a daddy to that boy.''

Tucker snorted. "You no more want to be a father to Tag than you want to work for a dollar.''

"Guess that don't really matter much, now does it?" Lambert replied with a superior lift of his chin. "Because the boy wants a daddy. And he wants it bad enough that it wouldn't take much for me to convince him you were the one that kept us apart."

He let that thought settle, then, seeing by the stricken look on Tucker's face that he'd accomplished what he'd set out to do, landed the final blow. "'Course, I suspect we could work us out a deal, if you really didn't want him to go."

Sara couldn't stand to see the pain on Tucker's face. She closed her eyes. She'd never hurt for anyone so badly in her life. His father. His own father had been using Tag to get to him, all the time waiting for the chance to take best advantage.

Stone-faced and solemn, Tucker had no choice but to play into his hand. "What's your price?"

"Can't put a price on a father's love for a son," Lambert said, sensing triumph and turning the screws.

"Don't push it, old man."

Seeing that he'd pressed Tucker to the limit, Lambert shrugged in concession. "Twenty ought to do—for now," he added with a greedy smile.

"You're out of your mind. I haven't got twenty grand."

"Then get it," he ordered bluntly.

In that moment, as Sara searched Tucker's face, she sensed that something snapped inside him. He seemed to age before her eyes as years of hatred, three decades of regret, caught up with him, too heavy a burden to fight any longer.

With a hunted look in his eyes, he turned to her.

"Do you see now why I can't have a future with you? Do you see the kind of cloth I'm cut from?

"Take a good look, Sara. Take a good look at my old man. People say I look just like him. People say I act just like him. He's a user, Sara. Take a good look!" he demanded, his voice rising to a pitch of raw humiliation and utter defeat. "Take a good long look, and remember—like father, like son."

Swallowing convulsively, he turned and faced his father head-on. "You're not getting one red cent from me. But you are leaving. If Tag wants to go with you, he's welcome to leave. Just make damn sure you're gone within the hour."

Then he turned and walked away.

"Don't you walk away from me, boy! I'm not through with you! You owe me, dammit! You owe me for that pretty-boy face you're so hot to show the ladies. You owe me for planting my seed in your mama and then marrying her when I'd just as soon walked away," Lambert yelled after Tucker.

His face had turned red and mottled with anger, his once handsome features twisted into an ugly caricature of a man who didn't know how to care.

Sara closed her eyes against the picture he made. Closed her eyes against the pain Tucker had to be feeling. A firm, determined voice had her opening them again.

"You heard my brother," Tag said, stepping out of the shadows. His face was haggard with sad acceptance, but his young man's eyes were hardened by an old man's failures. He shoved Lambert's beat-up duffel into his hand. "You'll leave here with what you came with, no more."

Wiping a trail of blood from his swollen lip, Lambert straightened his shoulders and smirked at his youngest son. "Thought you had more sense than him."

Tag looked at him long and hard. "And I thought you were something worth hanging on to."

A world of hurt clung to each precisely uttered word as Tag gave his father one last, empty look, then turned and walked away.

Lambert stood there, recovering his wind, rebuilding his swagger. When he turned to Sara, it was with venom in his eyes and acid on his tongue. "Has Tucker told you about the time he worked for your daddy?"

He snorted with ugly delight when her expression told him she didn't know what he was talking about.

"Ask him what happened," he said, with a hostile pleasure that had her insides churning with dread. "If he won't tell you about it, I'd bet the farm that your daddy'd be more'n happy to."

With one last vindictive look, he squared his shoulders, walked to his pickup and drove away.

Ten

Sara found Tucker in the shadows of the barn. He'd stripped off his shirt and was pitching hay with an agressiveness that had the horses nickering with restless uncertainty.

Pale alley light gilded the glistening planes of his bare back, defining muscle and sinew—and the tangible defeat that bowed his broad shoulders.

"He's gone," she said quietly.

He paused for a moment, then dug a little deeper into the pile and pitched a little faster. "Good. It'll save me from knocking the crap out of him."

"I think you'd have had to stand in line to do that."

He wiped a trickle of sweat from his brow with the back of a gloved hand and angled a look at her.

"Tag must have heard it all," she explained. "He gave him a less-than-gentle suggestion that he head for higher ground."

The relief in Tucker's eyes as he sucked in a deep breath, then turned back to the haystack, was a palpable thing. She knew then that she'd done the right thing in coming to him. Despite the unease churning in her belly over John Lambert's cryptic parting words, she'd had to let Tucker know he was gone. Tag had gone off to lick his own wounds. Lana would see to him. Tucker, as usual, was on his own.

And she was left wondering if she soon would be, too.

Tucker felt the fist that had been clenching in his gut ease up. He hadn't realized until now how much he'd been afraid of losing Tag. Tag and Lana and little Cody were as important to him as breathing. He didn't want to see them hurt. He didn't want to see them leave. But he would have let them go, because he loved them.

He had to let Sara go for the same reason.

"You were right about him."

Her words brought his head up.

"You were right about him," she repeated, when he remained silent. "But you were wrong about something else. You're nothing like him, Tucker. Nothing like him."

Gripping the pitchfork with both hands, he stuck the tines into the soft earth of the alley and closed his eyes.

"I didn't come out here to confront you," she said, moving up beside him, the resolve in her voice tinged with a reluctance she couldn't hide. "I came out here to ease your mind. But this can't wait any longer, can it?"

A long, tension-filled moment passed.

"What's happening with us, Tucker?"

The soft, searching look in her eyes was a grim reminder that he had to make her see he couldn't be a factor in her life.

"What's happening is that you need to let it go, Sara. Let it go," he repeated, letting a weary acceptance take over.

She approached him as a shy mare would approach an untested hand. "Because you've convinced yourself you aren't worth holding on to? Because you're so certain you're just like him?"

For the longest time, he didn't say anything. For the longest time, he couldn't. He just stood there, a muscle working in his jaw as he thought of his father, and his father's blood, running through his veins.

"Because all my life, I've known what a user he was. I've seen the effect he has on women. I saw it feed his ego. I saw it break my mother. And I see in your eyes that I have the power to do the same to you. I don't want the responsibility. I don't want to end up using you."

She smiled tentatively. "And you actually think I'd let you?"

He gave her a hard look. "I can't promise that I wouldn't try."

"Tucker—that's the most ridiculous crock of bull I've ever heard. In the first place, whether you choose to believe it or not, you've got too much integrity to do it. In the second, I'm strong enough to handle it if you did."

His look turned deep and probing. "Tell me something. Did my father leave here without bringing up your daddy and the fact that I once worked for him?"

She all but flinched as the certainty she'd been clinging to was nudged aside by unease.

He let a cynical smile lift one corner of his mouth. "I didn't think so. I didn't think he'd leave without firing that parting shot. And I can see that you want so much to believe in me that you sifted through his words and picked out only the things you wanted to hear."

"What I heard was an ugly and veiled accusation," she said, coming so quickly to his defense that his heart clenched. "What I heard was a selfish man trying to minimize the existence of a son he can't tolerate because he recognizes a better man when he sees one."

He swore under his breath, shaking his head. "Will you listen to yourself? You barely know me. Yet you're defending me without question. Just like my mother used to defend my father. Doesn't that tell you anything?"

She walked a step closer, her dark eyes glistening. "It tells me that I believe in you. It tells me that there is more to you as a man than you're willing to believe yourself."

With a deep breath and a prolonged look, he searched her face. Then, hooking his hands on his hips, he stared past her, digging for the words that would make her see.

"Tucker, we're good together," she went on, ignoring his dark silence. "We'd be great together, if you'd give it a chance. What's past is past. It has nothing to do with us now."

His heart was as hard as the set of his jaw when he finally spoke. "You just don't want to hear the truth, do you?"

She drew a ragged breath. "I want to hear whatever you want to tell me."

"I don't think so—but you're going to hear it anyway. You're lying when you say the past doesn't matter. *Your* past matters. It matters because you can't find it in you to talk to me about it.

"I wanted you to talk to me." He gritted the words out as the memory of that dark night came to him when, in the aftermath of treating the accident victim, she'd come apart in his arms but had refused to share her pain.

The cornered look in her eyes told him she knew exactly what he was talking about.

"I *needed* you to talk to me that night, Sara. I needed to know you trusted me. You couldn't do it."

She closed her eyes, hugging her arms tightly around her middle, the action an unconscious gesture of self-protection.

"You still can't," he added wearily. He hadn't realized until that moment how much her inability to trust him had been eating at him.

"This isn't about me," she insisted defensively. "It's about you, and how you feel about yourself."

He shook his head sadly. "You're wrong, Sara. You know you're wrong. Just like you know you don't really want to hear the truth about that ugly little story my father was dancing around."

His face grew hard as memories he didn't want to recall and truths he didn't like owning up to staked a claim on his consciousness.

"The old man wasn't blowing smoke. I was eighteen when I went to work for your daddy. I needed a job, and I was grateful as hell that he took me on. I learned about cutters that summer. How to read them. How to train them." He stopped, grim-faced. "What I didn't learn was how to stay clear of the boss's wife."

He watched her face as first denial, then unwilling acceptance, then weary revulsion, set in. She turned away from him, as if the very act could shut out his words. He snagged her arm and spun her around, making her face him.

"Your father's new little bride, Saundra, was restless and selfish and, yeah, she came on hard." He bit out the words, making her listen, driving the point home. "Pretty heady stuff for an eighteen-year-old who fancied himself a stud. That's when I figured out I was destined to act out the old man's legacy."

The imploring look in her eyes almost made him confess the rest. That he had fought it. That Saundra had threatened to have him fired if he didn't play her little game. That she had chased him and cornered him until finally he gave in and before long became drugged on the sex and the danger and her aggression, even as he hated himself because of his part in it.

"It was a lose-lose situation," he continued ruthlessly. "When your daddy finally caught on, she cried rape, and he ran me off with the business end of a twelve-gauge."

Her tears had begun to flow as the ugly truth took root. He made himself continue, knowing that every word was driving them further apart. Knowing that now she had to accept the extent of his weakness and the impossibility of any future together.

"Your father gave me a job, Sara. I repaid him by making time with his wife. Just like my old man. That's the kind of man you think you want to pin your hopes on."

His words had cut deep. So deep, he physically felt them rip through her slender body.

Feeling every inch the lowlife he was, he let her go when she pulled out of his grip. Feeling he deserved every wrenching twist that knotted in his chest and burned deep, he made himself watch as the best thing that had ever happened to him slowly walked away.

In the morning, when a grim-faced Tag drove her away from Blue Sky, he didn't try to say good-bye. He went to work. He focused on the cutter and the calf and the futurity. And he told himself it would be enough. Convinced himself it was more than he deserved.

Dallas was a lonely place. Sara stared out the window of Karla and Lance's high rise at the lights of the city. Pressing her forehead to the glass, she crossed her arms around her waist, fighting a wave of loneliness so pronounced it made her ache. She missed Cody. And Lana and Tag. She missed the ranch and the horses.

She missed Tucker.

"Earth to Sara."

She turned at the sound of Karla's voice. "I'm sorry. Did you say something?"

Karla gave her a mock scowl. "It's a good thing I'm secure with my sense of self, because you could sure convince a body in a hurry that they're as boring as white bread."

Sara forced a smile. "Sorry. Guess I'm a little preoccupied."

Karla tilted her head. "Interesting word, *preoccupied.* Encompasses so many things. Care to narrow down the possibilities?"

It was girls' night in. Lance was in New York on business, and after much pleading and cajoling, Karla had managed to convince Sara that she needed to come to dinner.

"Is it work?" Karla asked when Sara made no effort to elaborate.

Sara faced her squarely. "I handed in my resignation today."

Karla's face went pale before acceptance set in. "Well, I can't say I didn't expect it. I'm sorry. I'm sorry you couldn't work it out."

"I'm sorry, too. But I'm also relieved. Maybe I'm weak. Maybe I'm wrong not to tough it out. But I've lost the stomach for ER. I've lost my nerve. I can't count on myself to come through in a crisis anymore."

"Weakness has nothing to do with it, Sara. It's a matter of choice. At least it is for most of us. For you, I think, maybe it was a matter of proving yourself in your parents' eyes. The cause was right. The reasons were wrong. It happens. And you can't beat yourself up over it. Honey, if I ever said anything to make you think—"

"You haven't," Sara said, cutting her off. "You've never been anything but supportive. I was the one on the wrong track. It just took a while for it to sink in."

"So, what will you do?"

She turned back to the window, her look speculative. "I don't know. I do know that I'm a good nurse. I just need to get refocused on the reason I went into nursing in the first place. And I need a little more time." She thought of Lana, and the pleasure she'd felt when she was able to help her through a difficult spot. "Maybe I'll get into family practice. I think I can make a difference there."

"Yes," Karla agreed. "You can. But you aren't going to be good to anyone if you don't get this thing with Tucker settled."

One thing hadn't changed. She and Karla still shared everything. Karla knew the whole sordid story. Right up to the point when Sara had confronted her father with Tucker's confession. She'd always wondered what had happened between her father and his second wife. Their divorce had been quick and quiet. Her daddy never talked about it. Her mother had seemed content to gloat in a martyred silence.

When she finally worked up the nerve to confront him last week, her father had reluctantly filled her in. As it turned out, Tucker hadn't been Saundra's first less-than-discreet liaison. He'd been one of a string of many, for a woman who was practiced and proficient in the art of seduction. Especially the seduction of younger men. In the final windup, while there was no love lost between them and never would be, Paul Stewart figured Tucker had done him a favor.

In retrospect, Sara saw a young man already questioning his self-worth and an older woman convincing him with her attention that she could give him value.

She still felt for the child who had witnessed all that was bad in a role model. She hurt for the man whose sense of self-worth had been diminished by his father's example.

"Go to him, Sara."

Karla's voice was soft yet decisive, echoing the thoughts she'd battled in the two weeks since she'd left Blue Sky.

She remembered the look on Tucker's face when he'd told her. His blue eyes had been hardened by guilt, focused on good-bye.

''Go to him,'' Karla repeated when Sara met her eyes. ''Lance was right. He needs you.''

''Seems he's the only one who doesn't know that,'' she said brokenly.

Karla smiled. ''Then give him a reason to figure it out.''

The drive from Fort Worth to Blue Sky had been long and hot. After shooing Tag off to bed and checking with the new hand and making sure all was well with the stock, Tucker shut off the barn lights and stepped outside.

The moon was mellow and round. Like another moon on another night that his mind couldn't let go of. He could still see Sara by moonlight. Sometimes he could even convince himself he caught a hint of that light, exotic scent that was only hers and had, for a short time, been his.

Tonight was one of those times. He breathed deeply of the night as memories of heated skin and honeyed warmth stole through his body, adding to the ache of fatigue.

He even thought that if he stared hard enough and long enough into the darkness rimming the white board fence, he could make out her silhouette. Her dark hair, her slim, supple body, the night breeze rustling the folds of her flirty skirt against her long legs.

He could even hear her voice murmuring his name.

Awareness shot through him like an electric current as he made himself stop and stare and finally realize that it wasn't his mind playing games, or his eyes playing tricks.

She was there. In her tan bare feet, with her soft, uncertain smile, with her eyes aglow in the starlight and her heart balancing precariously on her sleeve.

"Hey, cowboy." She walked slowly toward him, her bare feet whispering across the Texas dust. She stopped in front of him, her brown eyes glittering with anticipation and anxiety and a palpable fear that he'd send her away.

That was exactly what he should do. He didn't have it in him. Couldn't make himself. He wanted to look and touch and hold her to him, shutting out the past, starting over in the present, and to hell with everything else.

There was so much he wanted to say. Yet he stood there like a post and finally heard himself utter, "What are you doing here?"

Her voice was as soft as the night breeze. "I think it falls in the category of a last-ditch effort."

He had to smile. If not because he was so damn glad to see her, then because of her tenacity.

"You were right about me, Tucker. I was asking you to accept the man I know you are, but I wasn't fulfilling my part of the bargain. I wasn't being up front with you. I was asking for everything and giving nothing back.

"I want a chance to fix that, if you'll let me."

He swallowed convulsively, wanting to take her in his arms so badly that he hurt with it. Wanting to believe she could mend all the things that were broken. But he had to face at least one unalterable fact.

"Some things can't be fixed, Sara." His past and her father's presence in it were a case in point.

"We all make mistakes, Tucker."

He closed his eyes and shook his head.

"I talked to my father. I got the whole story. Tucker, there are pieces even you don't know."

He gave her an uncertain look.

Her smile, if not full-fledged, was at least hopeful. "Let's just say that while I don't ever see the two of you as best friends, he's a reasonable man. He realizes people can change. And he's more tolerant than you'd think of youthful indiscretion—perhaps because Saundra was capable of pulling the wool over his eyes too. Maybe even because he's been guilty of some bad decisions in the past himself."

His chest tightened with an ache of regret and longing so strong he had to close his eyes against the pressure.

"Don't shut me out, Tucker. Please.

"I love you," she whispered, moving close, touching his arm, making him ache. "I want the chance to prove to you that I'm worth it, too."

He swallowed thickly. "Dammit, Sara, you're not making this easy."

"You catch on quick, cowboy," she murmured, with all the confidence he remembered and all the fire he wanted to claim.

It left him then. All the fight. All the denial. All of

his perfectly good intentions to protect her from everything bad he could give her.

"You'd better be sure about this—damn sure, darlin', because I haven't got it in me to fight you any longer."

Without another word, she flew into his arms. Without a hint of regret, he caught her.

"I've been so miserable," she murmured as she covered his face with kisses and buried her hands in his hair.

"I know."

"I've been so lonely." Her hands went to his shirt-front and ripped open the snaps.

He groaned as her cool hands touched his bare skin. "God, I know."

"I've been so horny," she moaned on a laugh as he lifted her fully against him and, chuckling with shared frustration and happiness, carried her toward the ranch house.

"Seems we are of the same mind, Miz Stewart."

"There's going to be a lot of that going around from now on, cowboy. Do you think you can get used to it?"

He shouldered open the door and stalked directly to his bedroom. "I think I'm going to love giving it a try."

With an urgency that held little regard for the sound of rent fabric or the give of delicate lace, they scrambled out of their clothes and fell together on the bed.

"I love you," he whispered as he eased himself into the silken haven of her body.

"Yes," she answered, urging him deep with her caress. "Yes, you do. And I'm not about to ever let you forget it."

Reason returned long, languid moments later. Tucker realized he must be crushing her. Weak and sweat-drenched, he rolled onto his side and pulled her against him to savor her nearness. He was spent. He was sated. He was in aching awe of the breadth and the depth of his physical need for her—in helpless acceptance of his love for her. In the undiluted joy of having her here in his arms.

He turned to look at her. Her expression was as soft as her sigh.

"No pressure, Tucker," she whispered, as if she felt the need to reassure him. "Whatever you can give me, that's what I'll accept. I won't crowd. I won't push. I just want the chance to see if we're up to this."

He lifted his hand to her hair, sifted its silken length through his fingers. "I don't know if I can be any good at this. I've convinced myself for so long that I'm just like him, it'll take awhile to shake loose of the expectations."

He rolled to his back, staring at the ceiling, remembering and sorting through. "For as long as I can remember, he was a rounder and a drifter. When he came home—if he came home—it was only when he felt like it. If he took care of us, it was more by accident than intent.''

A breath as thick as his memories and as heavy as his uncertainty escaped him.

''My best recollections of him are stumbling home drunk, picking a fight with my mother, and me shagging on to him when he went after her with his fists. And of Tag,'' he added after a long moment. ''He was four. Wide-eyed and crying, he'd cower in the corner, taking it all in.''

She said nothing. She just waited for him to finish.

''And then he'd leave. Be gone for weeks, months at a time. Once he was gone over a year. And every time, she'd take him back.

''I don't want that for us. I want what my little brother has. I want it all.''

His chest pounded as he turned to her. He searched her face in the cocooning darkness, needing to know she understood.

''I want it all,'' he repeated, understanding for the first time in his life how deeply that craving ate at him. ''And until you showed up, I was afraid to think it could ever happen. I'm still not sure I'll be any good at it.''

''That makes two of us who are unsure of ourselves,'' she said, her eyes glittering in the tender shadows. ''I'm scared, too, Tuck. Down to my toes. I'm scared you deserve more than what I can give you.

''No, let me finish,'' she insisted when he shook his head. ''You know all about duty and love and honor. You've shown that with what you've done for Tag and Lana. You've proven you're capable of all those things. I'm still uncharted ground.''

He understood then what she was trying to tell him. Understood the extent of her own reservations.

"Then chart a path for me, darlin','' he told her gently. "I want to know where you've been.''

She lowered her eyelids, her breath growing as deep as his own.

"It's not very pretty,'' she said after a long moment.

"I didn't expect it to be.''

He would have backed away then, when the silence lengthened and her hesitancy increased. No matter how important it was that she open up to him, he would have backed away. He felt her inner struggle. No matter how much it meant to him that she confide in him, he would not push her.

He'd decided this was as far as they were going to get when she started talking.

The words came slowly at first, spilling out of her like water, a little trickle at a time, then in a waterfall of broken memories and battered hopes, of mangled bodies and too-certain death.

"I think it was the futility of it all,'' she finally said, when she was spent. "The knowledge that one shift followed another, each one filled with the same victims of violent crime, the innocent caught in the cross fire, the young lives wasted for the colors of a gang.''

"I couldn't do it," he said, in awe of the horror she'd seen.

"Well, evidently, I couldn't, either. Only I was too stubborn to admit I was no longer in control."

He read the struggle in her eyes, saw the residual pain and knew the worst was yet to come.

"I should have known how deeply I was in trouble the day I walked by the drug cabinet and the thought crossed my mind that there lay the escape route."

He knew by the tightening of her body that she was bludgeoning herself with guilt.

"I don't know if I can explain it. The fact that I'd actually entertained, if only for a moment, the idea of resorting to drugs as an easy out was like awakening from a nightmare—or plunging headlong into one, I'm not sure which.

"I walked off the floor. I went home. And I just sort of turned off the switch. If the phone rang, I wouldn't answer. If someone came, I let them knock. I didn't eat. I didn't sleep. I didn't do anything but drink until a week later, when Karla convinced the super I was sick and he let her into the apartment."

He pulled her close against him, hurting for her, wanting more than he'd wanted anything in his life to shelter her.

"I recognize now that I'd reached a saturation point of sorts. I'm gradually accepting that that stunt I pulled was an involuntary defense mechanism, shutting my systems down before they overloaded. That doesn't make me proud, though, of the way I fell apart."

He ran his hand in a gentle caress up and down the length of her back. "I'm just glad that Karla and Lance had the sense to get you out of there. I'm glad you ended up at Blue Sky and that I was here to pick up the pieces."

She pulled back so that she could look in his eyes. "Me too," she whispered. "Me too."

"We're a pair, aren't we?" he said, nuzzling a kiss on the top of her head as she snuggled back against the warmth of his body.

"Two of a kind," she agreed. "We need each other, Tucker. And we can be good together. We just need to give it a chance."

Epilogue

The futurity in Fort Worth was the granddaddy of all cutting-horse competitions, with a total purse of over a million dollars. It was the culmination of eighteen months of training of the brightest and best three-year-olds from all over the world. It was the cherry at the top of the sundae. The summit of Mount Everest. The highest pie in the sky.

Sara was so nervous she wasn't sure she would keep her light lunch down when Tucker, aboard Poco, entered the round arena to the cheers of the crowd and the stoic, appraising eyes of the judges.

The pair had become a favorite of the cutting aficionados who had paid their money and packed into the Will Rogers Colosseum for the final night of competition.

Their style was crisp and thrilling. Their combined athleticism and grace awe-inspiring and natural. And the beauty of both horse and rider was unrivaled.

She'd gotten used to heads turning when Tucker made an entrance. She'd gotten accustomed to the glow she felt when he pulled her to his side and introduced her to his friends. But the pride she felt as she watched him and Poco warm up for the championship round was beyond any emotion in her experience.

Six months had passed since she'd returned to Blue Sky. Six months of sharing and loving. And healing. Both of them had had a lot of healing to do.

"They look revved."

This from Lana, who along with baby Cody shared the box seat at the rail of the arena and the excitement the moment promised.

"Let's hope they— Hey…" Sara paused, concern darkening her eyes as she studied Lana's face. "Are you okay? Maybe you should have sat this one out at the hotel."

Lana grinned, rubbed her fully extended tummy and lifted her brows. "And miss the night those two have been working toward for what seems like forever? Not on your life."

"I don't know," Sara insisted, second-guessing the wisdom of championing Lana's cause when she'd promised Dan Morton, Lana's obstetrician and Sara's new employer, that she'd keep a close rein on Lana's activities.

"Sara," Lana protested with a patient smile, "I'm

fine. And I've still got thirteen days to go, so relax. Besides, I went over with Cody. And little Elizabeth here," she continued, patting the baby still inside her, "she's a good girl. She wouldn't give her mama a hard time. Not tonight.

"Would you just look at them?" Lana continued, nodding toward Tucker on Poco and Tag, riding hold on the black filly he'd finally managed to talk Mason into selling him. "Aren't they just something, though?"

"Aren't they just?" Sara echoed, then drew a deep breath and tried to settle herself down. "It's show time."

The buzz of the crowd muted to a low murmur as the two-and-a-half-minute clock started and Tucker made his cut from the herd.

"Yes..." she hissed, her fingers balled into fists that she pressed against her mouth to keep from shouting as Poco made his first electrifying move on the calf. From then on, it just kept getting better. He dropped down on the calf, working hard as the determined Hereford tried him over and over again.

She watched the concentration on Tucker's face, knowing that despite the focused, firm set of his eyes, he was having the time of his life. Knowing that he'd enjoy it more when it was over and he had time to sit back and think about how fast and hard it was and how much acceleration there was in the run.

"You've got to put your mind in the horse's mind," she'd heard him tell Tag. "You've got to give up a little of yourself, and when you do, you feel all that power come up through your body and it becomes yours.''

The power was his tonight as they cut and dodged, getting ground with a sureness and speed that defined the sport at its finest, and the stallion showed Fort Worth what he was all about.

When the buzzer sounded, the entire arena erupted in an earsplitting roar. The crowd rose to their feet, yelling and whistling and showing their appreciation for the performance with a standing ovation.

The judges showed their appreciation too with a near-perfect 221-$\frac{1}{2}$ score that held up through the final contestant's performance and cinched first place in the most prestigious futurity in the world.

With tears of pride streaming down her cheeks, Sara latched hold of Cody's hand and, with special care for Lana's condition, maneuvered the three of them to ground level. Tag was so high he was practically floating when he spotted them making their way to the holding pen.

''Hot damn!'' he exclaimed, lifting Cody above his head and spinning him in a wild, fast circle. ''Did you see that, partner? Did you see Uncle Tuck show that old calf what for?''

Cody giggled and squealed for more as Tag lowered him to his hip and pulled Lana under his other arm for a hug. ''Ah, sugar, do you know what this means for Blue Sky?''

They all knew. It meant prestige, and revenue, and profit!

It also meant that Tucker was besieged by the

sports network commentators and a fair share of company reps wanting him to endorse everything from splint boots to saddles to underwear.

He tossed Sara a beleaguered but happy look over the heads of the mob huddled around him. She smiled hugely, mouthed a big "Way to go, cowboy!" and waited, her chest bursting with pride, while he basked in the glory of the moment.

It was nearly morning when they found their way back to their hotel room, deliriously happy and running on leftover adrenaline.

The door was barely shut behind them when Tucker spun her into his arms. "I never thought I'd get you alone," he growled, his back against the door, pulling her with him.

"You're a hot property now, Lambert," she said, arching her neck to make way for the soft, nuzzling kisses he strung along her jaw. "Better get used to it."

He raised his head, his smile so dazzling she felt fresh tears fill her eyes.

"He really showed 'em didn't he? That little stud proved there was a world-class engine to go along with all his chrome and polish. Did you hear what Murdock offered me for him?"

"I heard. I heard you turn him down, too."

"Hell, darlin', we'll make ten times that amount in breeding fees alone."

"Something tells me if you didn't stand to make a dime, you'd still be in this for the fun. I saw the look on your face tonight. You were having the time of your life."

"Not near as good a time as I'm going to show you." His grin was wicked and full of promise. "Why don't you go take your shower?"

When she returned to the bedroom, wrapped in a short robe and toweling her hair dry, she halfway expected to find Tucker asleep.

She was wrong. He was lying on the bed, his hands crossed behind his head, wearing nothing but a loose smile and tight latex.

"You are so easy," she said with a grin as she sank a knee into the mattress, beside him.

He reached for her. "And you are so glad." He ran his hand up under her robe, stroking the inside of her thigh, loving it when she shivered. "Come on down here."

"What'd you have in mind?" she asked, easing down beside him.

"Oh, I've got some special plans for you."

"Plans?"

"Plans to live up to my name. Hang on, little cowboy," he whispered, rolling her beneath him, "'cause I'm about to plum tucker you out."

She laughed and cradled his face in her hands. "I love it when you get all hokey with me."

"And I love it when you get that look in your eyes."

"What look?"

"That greedy look. The one that says you want me. The one that says you love me."

"Pretty sure of yourself, aren't you?"

"Yeah," he conceded, feeling a peace he'd never known. "For the first time in my life, I am.

"Marry me, Sara," he said, after an instant of hesitation.

If a heart could talk, hers was shouting. If eyes could speak, hers were babbling. If he would remember one word in his life as sacred, it was the fervent *Yes* she whispered that made his world complete.

* * * * * *

Escape to a place where a kiss is still a kiss...
Feel the breathless connection...
Fall in love as though it were
the very first time...
Experience the power of love!

Come to where favorite authors——such as
Diana Palmer, Stella Bagwell,
Marie Ferrarella and many more——
deliver heart-warming romance and genuine
emotion, time after time after time....

Silhouette Romance——
stories straight from the heart!

Silhouette®
Where love comes alive™